Praise for the *New York Times* bestseller

GWENDY'S BUTTON BOX

BY STEPHEN KING AND RICHARD CHIZMAR

"A different sort of coming-of-age story about a mysterious stranger and his odd little gift. . . . Cowritten with Richard Chizmar, King's zippy work returns to the small-town Maine locale of *The Dead Zone, Cujo* and other early novels. . . . extremely well-paced . . . a fun read that never loses momentum. . . . *Gwendy's Button Box* feels like it belongs in this locale that's always been a pit stop for scary Americana and the normal turned deadly. . . . Nicely captures that same winning dichotomy between the innocent and the sinister."
—*USA Today*

"Absorbing. . . . This bite-size gem of a story packs quite a punch."
—*Publishers Weekly*

"Man, I love this story! The whole thing just races and feels so right-sized and so scarily and sadly relevant. Loved the characters . . . and the sense of one little girl's connection to the whole world through this weird device. It all just sang."
—J. J. Abrams

D1114500

GWENDY'S MAGIC FEATHER

RICHARD CHIZMAR

GALLERY BOOKS

NEW YORK LONDON TORONTO SYDNEY NEW DELHI

Gallery Books
An Imprint of Simon & Schuster, Inc.
1230 Avenue of the Americas
New York, NY 10020

First Gallery Books trade paperback edition January 2020

GALLERY BOOKS and colophon are registered trademarks of Simon
& Schuster, Inc.

For information about special discounts for bulk purchases, please
contact Simon & Schuster Special Sales at 1-866-506-1949 or
business@simonandschuster.com

The Simon & Schuster Speakers Bureau can bring authors to your
live event. For more information or to book an event contact the
Simon & Schuster Speakers Bureau at 1-866-248-3049 or visit our
website at www.simonspeakers.com

Manufactured in the United States of America

10 9 8 7 6 5 4 3 2 1

Library of Congress Cataloging-in-Publication Data is available.

ISBN 978-1-9821-3972-8
ISBN 978-1-9821-3973-5 (ebook)

for Kara, Billy, and Noah
the Magic in my life

HOW GWENDY ESCAPED OBLIVION

by Stephen King

WRITING STORIES IS BASICALLY playing. Work may come into it once the writer gets down to brass tacks, but it almost always begins with a simple game of make-believe. You start with a what-if, then sit down at your desk to find out where that what-if leads. It takes a light touch, an open mind, and a hopeful heart.

Four or five years ago—I can't remember exactly, but it must have been while I was still working on the Bill Hodges trilogy—I started to play with the idea of a modern Pandora. She was the curious little girl, you'll remember, who got a magic box and when her damned curiosity (the curse of the human race) caused her to open it, all the evils of the world flew out. What would happen, I wondered, if a modern little girl got such a box, given to her not by Zeus but by a mysterious stranger?

I loved the idea and sat down to write a story called "Gwendy's Button Box." If you were to ask me where the name Gwendy came from, I couldn't tell you any more than I can tell you exactly when I did the original 20 or 30 pages. I might have been thinking about Wendy Darling, Peter Pan's little girlfriend, or Gwyneth Paltrow, or it might have just popped into my head (like the John Rainbird name did in *Firestarter*). In any case, I visualized a box with a colored button for each of the earth's large land masses; push one of them and something bad would happen in the corresponding continent. I added a black one that would destroy everything, and—just to keep the proprietor of the box interested—little levers on the sides that would dispense addictive treats.

I may also have been thinking of my favorite Fredric Brown short story, "The Weapon." In it, a scientist involved in creating a super-bomb opens his door to a late-night stranger who pleads with him to stop what he's doing. The scientist has a son who is, as we'd now say, "mentally challenged." After the scientist sends his visitor away, he sees his son playing with a loaded revolver. The final line of the story is, "Only a madman would give a loaded gun to an idiot."

Gwendy's button box is that loaded gun, and while she's far from an idiot, she's still just a kid, for God's sake. What would she do with that box, I wondered. How long would it take for her to get addicted to the treats it dispensed? How long before her curiosity caused her to push one of those buttons, just to see what might happen? (Jonestown, as it turned out.) And might she begin to be obsessed with the black button, the one that would destroy everything? Might the story end with Gwendy—after a particularly bad day, perhaps—pushing that button and bringing down the apocalypse? Would that be so farfetched in a world where enough nuclear firepower exists to destroy all life on earth for thousands of years? And where, whether we like to admit it or not, some of the people with access to those weapons are not too tightly wrapped?

The story went fine at first, but then I began to run out of gas. That doesn't happen to me often, but it *does* happen from time to time. I've probably got two dozen unfinished stories (and at least two novels) that just quit on me. (Or maybe I quit on them.) I think I was at the point where Gwendy is trying to figure out how to keep the box hidden from her parents. It all began to seem too complicated. Worse, I didn't know what came next. I stopped working on the story and turned to something else.

Time passed—maybe two years, maybe a little more. Every now and then I thought about Gwendy and her dangerous magic box, but no new ideas occurred, so the story stayed on the desktop of my office computer, way down in the corner of the screen. Not deleted, but definitely shunned.

Then one day I got an email from Rich Chizmar, creator and editor of Cemetery Dance and the author of some very good short stories in the fantasy/horror genre. He suggested—casually, I think, with no real expectation that I'd take him up on it—that we might collaborate on a story at some point, or that I might like to participate in a round-robin, where a number of writers work to create a single piece of fiction. The round-robin idea held no allure for me because such stories are rarely interesting, but the idea of collaboration did. I knew Rich's work, how good he is with small towns and middle-class suburban life. He effortlessly evokes backyard barbecues, kids on bikes, trips to Walmart, families eating popcorn in front of the TV . . . then tears a hole in those things by introducing an element of the supernatural and a tang of horror. Rich writes stories where the Good Life suddenly turns brutal. I thought if anyone could finish Gwendy's story, it would be him. And, I must admit, I was curious.

Long story short, he did a brilliant job. I re-wrote some of his stuff, he re-wrote some of mine, and we came out with a little gem. I'll always be grateful to him for not allowing Gwendy to die a lingering death in the lower righthand corner of my desktop screen.

When he suggested there might be more to her story,

I was interested but not entirely convinced. What would it be about? I wanted to know. He asked me what I'd think if Gwendy, now an adult, got elected to the United States House of Representatives, and the button box made a reappearance in her life . . . along with the box's mysterious proprietor, the man in the little black hat.

You know when it's right, and that was so perfect I was jealous (not a lot, but a little, yeah). Gwendy's position of power in the political machinery echoed the button box. I told him that sounded fine, and he should go ahead. In truth, I probably would have said the same if he'd suggested a story where Gwendy becomes an astronaut, goes through a space warp, and ends up in another galaxy. Because Gwendy is as much Rich's as she is mine. Probably more, because without his intervention, she wouldn't exist at all.

In the story you're about to read—lucky you!—all of Rich's formidable skills are on display. He evokes Castle Rock well, and the regular Joes and regular Jills that populate the town ring true. We know these people, and so we care for them. We also care for Gwendy. To tell you the truth, I sort of fell in love with her, and I'm delighted that she's back for more.

Stephen King
May 17, 2019

ON THURSDAY, DECEMBER 16, 1999, Gwendy Peterson wakes up before the sun, dresses in layers for the cold, and heads out for a run.

Once upon a time, she walked with a slight limp thanks to an injury to her right foot, but six months of physical therapy and orthotic inserts in her favorite New Balance running shoes took care of that little problem. Now she runs at least three or four times a week, preferably at dawn as the city is just beginning to open its eyes.

An awful lot has happened in the fifteen years since Gwendy graduated from Brown University and moved away from her hometown of Castle Rock, Maine, but there's plenty of time to tell that story. For now, let's tag along as she makes her way crosstown.

After stretching her legs on the concrete steps of her rented townhouse, Gwendy jogs down Ninth Street, her feet slapping a steady rhythm on the salted roadway, until it runs into Pennsylvania Avenue. She hangs a sharp left and cruises past the Navy Memorial and the National Gallery of Art. Even in the heart of winter, the museums are all well illuminated, the gravel and asphalt walkways shoveled clean; our tax dollars hard at work.

Once Gwendy reaches the Mall, she notches it up a gear, feeling the lightness in her feet and the power in her legs. Her ponytail peeks out from underneath her winter cap, rustling against the back of her sweatshirt with every step she takes. She runs along the Reflecting Pool, missing the families of ducks and birds that make it their home during the warm summer months, toward the obelisk shadow of the Washington Monument. She stays on the lighted path, swinging a wide circle around the famous landmark, and heads east toward the Capitol Building. The Smithsonian Museums line both sides of the Mall here and she remembers the first time she visited Washington, D.C.

She was ten that summer, and she and her parents spent three long, sweaty days exploring the city from dawn to dusk. At the end of each day, they collapsed on their hotel beds and ordered room service—an unheard of luxury for the Peterson family—because they were too exhausted to shower and venture out for dinner. On their final morning, her father surprised the family with tickets to one of the city's pedi-cab tours. The three of them squeezed into the back of the cramped carriage eating ice cream cones and giggling as their tour guide pedaled them around the Mall.

Never in a million years did Gwendy dream she'd one day live and work in the nation's capital. If anyone questioned her of that likelihood even eighteen months earlier, her answer would have been a resounding no. *Life is funny that way,* she thinks, cutting across a gravel pathway in the direction of Ninth Street. Full of surprises—and not all of them good.

Leaving the Mall behind, Gwendy pulls frigid air into her lungs and quickens her stride for the final home stretch. The streets are alive now, bustling with early morning commuters, homeless people emerging from their cardboard boxes, and the rumble and grind of garbage trucks making their rounds. Gwendy spots the multi-colored Christmas lights twinkling from her bay window ahead and takes off in a sprint. Her neighbor across the street lifts a hand and calls out to her, but Gwendy doesn't see or hear. Her legs flex with fluid grace and strength, but her mind is far away this cold December morning.

EVEN WITH DAMP HAIR and barely a hint of make-up on her face, Gwendy is gorgeous. She draws a number of appreciative—not to mention a few openly envious—stares as she stands in the corner of the cramped elevator. Were her old friend, Olive Kepnes, still alive (even after all these years Gwendy still thinks of her almost every day), Olive would tell Gwendy that she looked like a million bucks and change. And she would be right.

Dressed in plain gray slacks, a white silk blouse, and low-heeled slip-ons (what her mother calls sensible shoes), Gwendy looks ten years younger than her thirty-seven years. She would argue vigorously with anyone who told her so, but her protests would be in vain. It was the simple truth.

The elevator dings and the doors slide open onto the third floor. Gwendy and two others sidestep their way out and join a small group of employees waiting in line at a cordoned-off security checkpoint. A burly guard wearing a badge and side-arm stands at the entrance, scanning identification badges. A young female guard is positioned a few yards behind him, staring at a video screen as employees pass between the verti-cal slats of a walk-through metal detector.

When it's Gwendy's turn at the front of the line, she pulls a laminated ID card from her leather tote bag and hands it to the guard.

"Morning, Congresswoman Peterson. Busy day today?" He scans the bar code and hands it back with a friendly smile.

"They're all busy, Harold." She gives him a wink. "You know that."

His smile widens, exposing a pair of gold-plated front teeth. "Hey, I won't tell if you don't."

Gwendy laughs and starts to walk away. From behind her: "Tell that husband of yours I said hello."

She glances over her shoulder, readjusting the tote bag on her arm. "Will do. With any luck, he'll be home in time for Christmas."

"God willing," Harold says, crossing himself. Then he turns to the next employee and scans his card. "Morning, Congressman."

3

GWENDY'S OFFICE IS SPACIOUS and uncluttered. The walls are painted a soft yellow and adorned with a framed map of Maine, a square silver-edged mirror, and a Brown University pendant. Bright, warm lighting shines down on a mahogany desk centered along the opposite wall. Atop the desk are a hooded lamp, telephone, day-planner, computer and keyboard, and numerous stacks of paperwork. Across the room is a dark leather sofa. A coffee table covered with fanned-out magazines sits in front of it. A small table with a coffee station stands off to one side. There's also a three-drawer filing cabinet in the far corner and a small bookshelf lined with hardcover books, knickknacks, and framed photographs. The first of the two largest photos shows a tan and beaming Gwendy standing arm-in-arm with a handsome bearded man at the Castle Rock Fourth of July parade two years earlier. The second is of a much younger Gwendy standing in front of her mother and father at the base of the Washington Monument.

Gwendy sits at her desk, chin resting atop interlocked hands, staring at the photograph of her and her parents instead of the report sitting open in front of her. After a moment, she sighs and closes the folder, pushing it aside.

She taps a flurry of buttons on the keyboard and opens her email account. Scanning the dozens of notices in her mailbox, she stops on an email from her mother. The time-code shows it was received ten minutes earlier. She double-clicks on it and a digital scan of a newspaper article fills her monitor screen.

The Castle Rock Call
Thursday – December 16, 1999
STILL NO SIGN OF TWO MISSING GIRLS

Despite a countywide search and dozens of tips from concerned citizens, there has been no progress in the case of two abducted Castle County girls.

The latest victim, Carla Hoffman, 15, of Juniper Lane in Castle Rock, was taken from her bedroom on the evening of Tuesday, December 14. At shortly after six p.m., her older brother walked across the street to visit a classmate from school. When he returned home no more than fifteen minutes later, he discovered the back door broken open and his sister missing.

"We're working around the clock to find these girls," Castle Rock Sheriff Norris Ridgewick commented. "We've brought in officers from neighboring towns and are organizing additional searches."

Rhonda Tomlinson, 14, of nearby Bridgton, vanished on her way home from school on the afternoon of Tuesday, December 7...

Gwendy frowns at the computer screen. She's seen enough. She closes the email and starts to turn away—but hesitates. Tapping at the keyboard, she switches to SAVED MAIL and uses the Arrow button to scroll. After what feels like forever, she stops on another email from her mother, this one dated November 19, 1998. The subject line reads: CONGRATULATIONS!

She opens it and double-clicks on a link. A small, dark window with *Good Morning, Boston* written across it opens at the center of the monitor. Then a low resolution video comes to life and the *Good Morning, Boston* intro music is blaring from the computer speakers. Gwendy quickly turns down the volume.

Onscreen, Gwendy and popular morning show host, Della Cavanaugh, sit across from each other on straight-backed leather chairs. They each have their legs crossed and are wearing microphones clipped to their collars. A banner head-line runs across the top of the video screen: HOMETOWN GIRL MAKES GOOD.

Gwendy cringes at the sound of her voice on the video, but she doesn't turn it off. Instead, she readjusts the volume, leans back in her chair, and watches herself being interviewed, remembering how utterly strange—and unsettling—it felt to tell her life story to thousands of strangers . . .

4

AFTER GRADUATING FROM BROWN in the spring of 1984, Gwendy spends the summer working a part-time job in Castle Rock before attending the Iowa Writers Workshop in early September. For the next three months, she focuses on classwork and starts writing the opening chapters of what will become her first novel, a multi-generational family drama set in Bangor.

When the workshop is over, she returns home to Castle Rock for the holidays, gets a tattoo of a tiny feather next to the scar on her right foot (more about that feather a little later), and begins to search for full-time employment. She receives a number of interesting offers and soon after decides on an upstart advertising and public relations firm in nearby Portland.

In late January 1985, Mr. Peterson follows behind Gwendy on the interstate—pulling a U-Haul trailer full of secondhand furniture, cardboard boxes stuffed with clothes, and more shoes than any one person should own—and helps her move into a rented second-floor downtown apartment.

Gwendy begins work the following week. She quickly proves to be a natural at the advertising game and over the course of the next eighteen months, earns a couple of promotions. By the middle of year two, she's traveling up and down the east coast to meet with VIP clients and is listed on company letterhead as an Executive Account Manager.

Despite her hectic schedule, the unfinished novel is never

far from Gwendy's mind. She daydreams about it constantly and pecks away at it in every nook and cranny of free time she can muster: long flights, weekends, infrequent snow days, and the occasional weeknight when her workload allows.

At a holiday work party in December 1987, her boss, making polite conversation, introduces Gwendy to an old college friend and mentions that his star employee is not only a first-class account manager, but also an aspiring author. The old friend just happens to be married to a literary agent, so he calls his wife over and introduces her to Gwendy. Relieved to have a fellow book lover to talk to, the agent takes an immediate liking to Gwendy and by the end of the night, she convinces the aspiring author to send her the first fifty pages of her manuscript.

When the second week of January rolls around and Gwendy's phone rings one afternoon, she's shocked to find the agent on the line inquiring as to the whereabouts of those first fifty pages. Gwendy explains that she'd figured the agent was just being courteous and she didn't want to add one more unpublishable book to the slush pile. The agent assures Gwendy that she's never courteous when it comes to her reading material and insists that she send it right away. So, later that day, Gwendy prints the first three chapters of her novel, stuffs them into a FedEx overnight envelope and sends them on their way. Two days later, the agent calls back and asks to see the rest of the manuscript.

There's only one problem: Gwendy isn't finished writing the book.

Instead of admitting this to the agent, she takes the following day, a Friday, off from work—a first for Gwendy—and spends a long weekend drinking Diet Pepsi by the gallon and writing her ass off to finish the last half-dozen chapters.

During her lunch break on Monday, Gwendy prints the almost three hundred remaining pages of the book and crams them into a FedEx box.

Several days later, the agent calls and offers to represent Gwendy. The rest, as they say, is history.

In April 1990, twenty-eight-year-old Gwendy Peterson's debut novel, *Dragonfly Summer*, is published in hardcover to rave reviews and less than impressive sales. A few months later, it wins the prestigious Robert Frost Award, given annually "to a work of exemplary literary merit" by the New England Literary Society. This honor sells maybe—and that's a hard *maybe*—a few hundred extra copies and makes for a nice cover blurb on the paperback edition. In other words, it's nothing to take to the bank.

That all changes soon enough with the release of Gwendy's second book, a suburban thriller called *Night Watch*, published the following autumn. Stellar reviews and strong word-of-mouth sales rocket it onto the *New York Times* bestseller list for four consecutive weeks, where it rests comfortably amidst mega-sellers by Sidney Sheldon, Anne Rice, and John Grisham.

The following year, 1993, sees the publication of Gwendy's third and most ambitious novel, *A Kiss in the Dark*, a hefty six-hundred-page thriller set on a cruise ship. The book earns a return trip to the bestseller list—this time for six weeks—and soon after the film version of *Night Watch* starring Nicolas Cage as the cuckolded suburban husband hits theaters just in time for the holidays.

At this point in her career, Gwendy's poised to make the leap to the big leagues of the entertainment industry. Her agent anticipates a seven-figure offer in the next book auction, and both *Dragonfly Summer* and *A Kiss in the Dark* are now deep in development by major film studios. All she has to do is stay the course, as her father likes to say.

Instead, she changes direction and surprises everyone.

A Kiss in the Dark is dedicated to a man named Johnathon Riordan. Years earlier, when Gwendy started working at the ad agency, it was Johnathon who took her under his wing and taught her the ropes of the advertising world. At a time when he could've easily viewed her as direct competition—especially with their proximity in age; Johnathon only being three years older than Gwendy—he instead befriended her and grew to become her closest ally, both in and outside the office. When Gwendy locked her keys in the car for the second time in as many days, whom did she call for help? Johnathon. When she needed serious dating advice, whom did she summon? Johnathon. The two of them spent countless evenings after work eating Chinese food straight out of the carton and watching romantic comedies at Gwendy's apartment. When Gwendy sold her debut novel, Johnathon was the first person she told, and when she did her first book signing, he was standing at the front of the line at the bookstore. As time passed and their relationship grew closer, Johnathon became the big brother Gwendy never had but always wanted. And then he got sick. And nine months later, he was gone.

This is where the surprise enters the picture.

Inspired by the AIDS-related death of her best friend, Gwendy resigns from the ad agency and spends the next eight months writing a non-fiction memoir about Johnathon's inspiring life as a young gay man and the tragic circumstances of his passing. When she's finished, still not over the heartbreak, she immediately pours herself into directing a documentary based on Johnathon's story.

Family and friends are surprised, but not surprised. Most

seem to explain her newfound passion with the simple, well-worn statement: "That's just Gwendy being Gwendy." As for her agent, although she never comes right out and says it—that would be unsympathetic, not to mention unkind—she is profoundly disappointed. Gwendy had been on the fast track to stardom and had veered off to tackle a topic as controversial and unseemly as the AIDS epidemic.

But Gwendy doesn't care. Someone important once told her: "You have many things to tell the world . . . and the world will listen." And Gwendy Peterson believes that.

Eyes Closed: Johnathon's Story is published in the summer of 1994. It garners positive reviews in *Publishers Weekly* and *Rolling Stone*, but is a slow mover in the national bookstore chains. By the end of August, it's demoted to bargain bins in the back of most stores.

The similarly titled documentary is another story altogether. Released shortly after the book, the film plays to packed festival audiences and goes on to win an Academy Award for Best Documentary. Nearly fifty million viewers watch as Gwendy gives her tearful acceptance speech. She spends the majority of the next few months doing interviews with national publications and appearing on various morning and late-night talk shows. Her agent is over the moon. She's back on the fast track again and more in demand than ever before.

Gwendy first meets Ryan Brown, a professional photographer from Andover, Massachusetts, during the making of the *Eyes Closed* documentary. The two strike up an easy friendship and, in an unforeseen turn of events for both, it grows into a relationship.

On a cloudless November morning, while hiking along the banks of the Royal River near Castle Rock, Ryan pulls a diamond ring out of his backpack, gets down on a knee, and proposes. Gwendy, tears and snot streaming down her face, is so caught up in the moment she finds herself unable to utter a single word. So, Ryan, ever the good sport, shifts to his other knee and asks again. "I know how much you like surprises, Gwennie. C'mon, what do you say? Spend the rest of your life with me?" This time Gwendy finds her voice.

They're married the following year at her parents' church in the center of Castle Rock. The reception is held at the Castle Inn and, despite Ryan's younger brother drinking too much and breaking his ankle on the dance floor, a good time is had by all. The father of the bride and the father of the groom bond over their mutual admiration of Louis L'Amour oaters, and the two mothers spend the entire day giggling like sisters. Most folks predict now that Gwendy is hitched, she'll settle down and concentrate on writing novels again.

But Gwendy Peterson does love surprises—and she has one more up her sleeve.

Born of simmering anger and frustration at the cruel and discriminatory manner in which many AIDS victims continue to be treated (she's particularly incensed that Congress recently voted to retain a ban on entry into the country for people living with HIV, even as more than two-and-a-half million AIDS cases have been reported globally), Gwendy decides—with her husband's blessing—to run for public office.

Suffice to say, her agent is not pleased.

Gwendy pours her heart and soul into a grassroots campaign, and it quickly catches fire. Volunteers show up in unprecedented numbers and early fund-raisers exceed all expectations. As one notoriously stingy pundit notes: "Peterson, with boundless charisma and energy to match, has

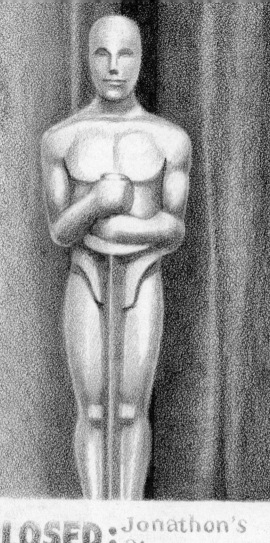

Peterson   **EYES CLOSED**: Jonathon's Story   Scribner

not only managed to mobilize the young vote and the unde-cided vote, she's found a way to stir the merely curious. And, in a state as tradition-steeped as Maine, that may well prove to be the key to a successful fall."

It turns out he's right. In November 1998, by a margin of less than four thousand votes, Gwendy Peterson upsets incumbent Republican James Leonard for the District One Congressional Seat of Maine. The following month, just days after Christmas, she makes the move to Washington, D.C.

So, there you have it, the story of how Gwendy finds herself eleven months and eight days into a two-year Congressional term, peddling her idealistic ideologies (as Fox News referred to them during last night's broadcast) to any-one who will listen, and often being referred to—with a not so subtle hint of derision—as the Celebrity Congresswoman.

The intercom on her desk buzzes, yanking Gwendy out of her time machine. She fumbles with the keyboard, clos-ing the video window on her computer screen, and presses a blinking button on her telephone. "Yes?"

"Sorry to disturb, but you have a meeting with Rules and Records in seven minutes."

"Thanks, Bea. I'll be right out."

Gwendy glances at her wristwatch in disbelief. *Jesus, you just woolgathered away forty-five minutes of your morning. What's wrong with you?* It's a question she's asked herself a lot lately. She grabs a pair of manila folders from the top of the stack and hurries out of the office.

5

As is often the case in this corner of the world, an earlier meeting is running late, so Gwendy arrives with plenty of time to spare. Nearly two dozen House Representatives are crammed into the narrow hallway waiting to enter Conference Room C-9, so she positions herself by the water cooler in the outer lobby, hoping to review her notes in private. No such luck—it's been that kind of morning.

"Forget to do your homework last night, young lady?"

She clenches her jaw and looks up from the open folder.

Milton Jackson, longtime representative of the state of Mississippi, is seventy years old, looks ninety, and is the spitting image of what a buzzard would look like if it fluttered down from a telephone wire and slipped on a Men's Wearhouse suit. In other words, not pretty.

"Of course not," Gwendy says, offering her brightest smile. From day one at her new job, she recognized that Milton was one of those men who loathed anyone with a positive outlook on life or was simply happy, so she really turns it on. "Just doing some extra credit. And how are you this fine December morning?"

The old man squints at her, as if he's trying to figure out if it was a trick question. "Ahh, I'm okay," he finally grumbles.

"Leave her alone, Milt," someone says from behind them. "She's young enough to be your granddaughter."

This time Gwendy's smile is genuine as she turns to her

friend. "I'd know that sweet voice anywhere. Good morning, Patsy."

"Heya, Gwennie. This old coot bothering you?" Patsy Follett is in her mid-sixties and as cute as she is petite. Even in the stylish high-heeled boots she's wearing, Patsy stands barely five feet tall. Her bobbed hair is dyed platinum and her make-up is, shall we say, plentiful.

"No, ma'am, we were just talking strategy for today's meeting." She looks at the congressman. "Isn't that right, Mr. Jackson?"

The old man doesn't respond. Just studies them from behind thick eyeglasses like they're flying insects splattered against the windshield of his brand new Mercedes.

"Speaking of strategy," Patsy says. "You still owe me a return call on that education budget, Milt."

"Yeah, yeah," he grumbles. "I'll have my secretary get back to you with a date."

Gwendy glances down at the floor and notices a piece of toilet paper stuck to the heel of one of the old man's loafers. She carefully reaches out with the tip of her shoe and nudges it free. Then, she slides the toilet paper against the wall so no one else will step on it.

"Or maybe you could just pick up the phone all by yourself and call me back later today," Patsy says, arching her eyebrows.

Milton scowls and elbows his way toward the front of the crowd without so much as a goodbye.

Patsy watches him go and lets out a thin whistle. "Boy, that ugly mug of his is enough to make you want to skip breakfast. Maybe lunch, too."

Gwendy's eyes widen and she tries to hold back a giggle. "Be nice."

"An impossibility, dear girl. I am cranky as a hornet today."

A murmur ripples through the crowd and they finally start inching toward the entrance of the conference room.

"Guess it's that time again," Patsy says.

Gwendy puts out a hand, gesturing for her friend to go ahead of her. "What time is that?"

Patsy smiles, and her tiny, make-up–laden face lights up. "Time to fight the good fight, of course."

Gwendy sighs and follows her friend inside.

6

Two hours later, the door to the conference room bangs open and thirty representatives stream out, every last one of them looking like they could use a handful of Tylenol or, at the very least, a cold shower.

"Did you see Old Man Henderson's face?" Patsy asks as she and Gwendy enter the hallway. "I thought he was going to blow a gasket right there at the podium."

"I never saw anyone get so red—"

Someone bumps Gwendy hard from behind, knocking her aside, and keeps on hustling past. It's their chatty friend from this morning, Milton Jackson.

"Hey, nice manners, asshole," Patsy calls after him.

Gwendy tucks the manila folders under her arm and rubs her shoulder.

"You okay?"

"Oh, I'm fine," she says. "You shouldn't have yelled at him like that."

"Why not? The guy deserved it." She gives Gwendy a look. "You're not very good at losing your temper, are you?"

Gwendy shrugs. "I guess not."

"You should try it sometime. Might make you feel better."

"Fine. Next time that happens I'll call him . . . a walking example of why we need term limits."

"Sshhh," Patsy says, as they file into the elevator. "You're one of us now."

Gwendy laughs and presses the button for their floor.

"Any movement with the pharmaceutical people?" Patsy asks.

Gwendy shakes her head and lowers her voice. "Ever since Columbine everyone has shifted to gun control and mental health. And how can I blame folks for that? I just wish people around here had longer attention spans than kindergarteners. Three months ago, I almost had the votes. Today, it's not even close."

The elevator door slides open and they walk out into a mostly empty lobby. "Welcome to the grind, girlfriend. It'll circle back around. It always does."

"How long have you been doing this, Patsy?"

"I've represented the second district of the honorable state of South Carolina for sixteen years now."

Gwendy whistles. "How . . . ?" She pauses.

"How do I do it?"

Gwendy nods shyly.

Patsy puts a hand on the young congresswoman's shoulder. "Listen, honey, I know what you're thinking. How did you get yourself into this mess? It's not even been a year and you're frustrated and overwhelmed and looking for a way out."

Gwendy looks at her, saucer-eyed. "That's not what I—"

Patsy waves her off. "Trust me, we all went through it. It'll pass. You'll find your groove. And if you don't and you find your head slipping under water, give me a call. We'll find a way to fix it together."

Gwendy leans over and hugs her friend. It's a little like embracing a child, she thinks. "Thank you, Patsy. I swear you're an angel."

"I'm really not. I'm old and fussy and don't much care

21

for most of humanity, but you're different, Gwennie. You're special."

"I don't feel very special these days, but thank you again. So much."

Patsy starts to walk away, but Gwendy calls after her. "You really meant it? You've felt like this before?"

Patsy turns and puts her hands on her hips. "Honey, if I had a nickel for every time I've felt the way you're feeling, I still wouldn't have change for a quarter."

Gwendy bursts out laughing. "What does that even mean?"

Patsy shrugs her shoulders. "Beats me. My late husband used to say it whenever he wanted to sound clever and it's stuck with me ever since."

7

GWENDY WALKS INTO HER outer office feeling better than she has in days. It's almost as if a weight has been lifted from her chest and she can breathe again.

A gray-haired receptionist stops typing and looks up from her computer screen. "I left two messages on your desk and lunch should be here soon. Turkey club and chips okay?"

If Gwendy sometimes envisions (secretly, of course; she would never say these things out loud, not in a million years) Representative Patsy Follett as Tinkerbell, the wand-waving, miniature flying guardian angel of her childhood, then she most certainly imagines her receptionist, Bea Whiteley, as Sheriff Taylor's beloved Aunt Bea from the iconic television series, *The Andy Griffith Show*.

Although there's very little physical resemblance (for starters, Gwendy's Bea is African-American), there are a multitude of other similarities. First, there's the name, of course. How many women do you know named Bea or even Beatrice? And then there're the indisputable facts: Mrs. Whiteley is a natural caregiver, an outstanding cook, a person of devoted faith, and the sweetest, most good-natured woman Gwendy has ever known. Wrap all that up into a single human being and who do you have? Aunt Bea, that's who.

"You're a lifesaver," Gwendy says. "Thank you."

Bea picks up a sheet of paper from the corner of her desk. "I also printed your schedule for tomorrow." She gets up and hands it to Gwendy.

The congresswoman scans it with a frown. "Why does this feel like the last day of school before Christmas break?"

"Pretty sure the last day of school was a lot more fun than this." Bea sits down at her desk again. "How's your mom feeling?"

"Still good as of last night. Six weeks out from chemo. Markers in the normal range."

The older lady clasps her hands together. "God is good."

"Dad's driving her crazy, though. Want to hear the latest?" She doesn't wait for an answer. "He wants to withdraw all their savings and bury it in the back yard. He's convinced the bank's computer system's going to crash because of Y2K. Mom can't wait for him to start back at work again."

"All the more reason for you to get home. You flying out tomorrow night?" Bea asks.

Gwendy shakes her head. "Bumped my flight until Saturday morning. I need to wrap up a couple things before I go. How about you? When are you and Tim headed out?"

"We leave Monday to visit my sister in Colorado, and from there we go to see the kids on Wednesday. Speaking of the kids . . . would it be too much trouble to ask you to sign a couple of books for them? I'm happy to pay. I'm not asking for them for free or—"

Gwendy puts her hand out. "Will you please hush? I'd be happy to, Bea. It'd be my pleasure."

"Thank you, Mrs. Peterson. I'm very grateful." And she looks it, too, not to mention, relieved.

"Just go relax and enjoy that family of yours."

"All of us under the same roof for an entire week? It should be . . . interesting."

"It'll be a blast," Gwendy says.

Bea rolls her eyes. "If you say so."

"I say so." She walks into her office, laughing, and closes the door behind her.

8

GWENDY TOSSES THE REPORTS back onto the stack and sits at her desk. She reaches for her day-planner, but her hand freezes in mid-air before it gets there.

There's a shiny silver coin sitting next to the keyboard.

Her outstretched hand begins to tremble. Her heart thumps in her chest, and it suddenly feels as if all the air has been sucked out of the room.

She knows before she looks that it's an 1891 Morgan silver dollar. She's seen them before.

A familiar voice, a man's voice, whispers in her ear: *"Almost half an ounce of pure silver. Created by Mr. George Morgan, who was just thirty years old when he engraved the likeness of Anna Willess Williams, a Philadelphia matron, to go on what you'd call the 'heads' side of the coin..."*

Gwendy whips her head around, but no one is there. She glances about her office, waiting for the voice to return, feeling as if she's just seen a ghost—and maybe she has. Nothing else in the room appears out of place. Reaching out with her other hand, she lets the tip of her index finger brush against the surface of the coin. It's cool to the touch, and it's real. She's not imagining it. She's not suffering some kind of stress-induced mental breakdown.

Heart in her throat, Gwendy uses her thumb to slowly slide the coin across the desk, closer to her. Then she leans down for a better look. The silver dollar is in mint condition

and she was right—it's an 1891 Morgan. Anna Williams smiles up at her with unblinking silver eyes.

Pulling her hand back, Gwendy absently wipes it on the sleeve of her blouse. She gets up then and slowly wanders around the room, feeling as if she's just awakened from a dream. She bangs her knee against the rounded corner of the coffee table but she barely notices. Abruptly changing direction, she stops in front of the closet door, the only place where someone could possibly hide. After taking a steadying breath, she silently counts to three—and yanks open the door.

She recoils with her hands held in front of her face, nearly falling, but there's no one waiting inside. Just a handful of coats and sweaters hanging on wire hangers, a tangle of dress and running shoes littering the floor, and a brand-new pair of snow boots still in the box.

Exhaling with relief, Gwendy pushes the door shut and turns to face her desk again. The silver coin sits there, gleaming in the overhead lights, staring back at her. She's about to call for Bea when something catches her eye. She crosses to the filing cabinet in the corner. A bronze bust of Maine Civil War hero Joshua Chamberlain sits on top of it, a gift from her father.

Gwendy pulls open the top drawer of the cabinet. It's stuffed with folders and assorted paperwork. She closes it. Then she does the same with the second drawer: slides it open, quick inspection, close. Holding her breath, she bends to a knee and pulls open the bottom drawer.

And there it is: the button box.

A beautiful mahogany, the wood glowing a brown so rich that she can glimpse tiny red glints deep in its finish. It's about fifteen inches long, maybe a foot wide, and half that deep. There are a series of small buttons on top of the box, six in rows of two, and a single at each end. Eight in all. The pairs are light green and dark green, yellow and orange, blue and violet. One of the end-buttons is red. The other is black. There's also a small lever at each end of the box, and what looks like a slot in the middle.

For a moment, Gwendy forgets where she is, forgets how old she is, forgets that a kind and gentle man named Ryan Brown was ever born. She's twelve years old again, crouching in front of her bedroom closet back in the small town of Castle Rock, Maine.

It looks exactly the same, she thinks. *It looks the same because it* is *the same.* There's no mistaking it even after all these years.

From behind her, there's a loud knock at the door. Gwendy almost faints.

9

"ARE YOU OKAY, CONGRESSWOMAN? I was knocking for a long time."

Gwendy steps back from the door and lets her receptionist into the office. Bea's carrying a small tray with the turkey club lunch on it. She places it on the desk and turns back to her boss. If Bea notices the silver coin sitting next to the keyboard, she doesn't mention it.

"I'm fine," Gwendy says. "Just a little embarrassed. I was doing some reading and I guess I dozed off."

"Must've been some dream you were having. It sounded like you were whimpering."

You don't know the half of it, Gwendy thinks.

"You sure you're okay?" Bea asks. "If you don't mind my saying, you look a little rattled and a lot pale. Almost like you've seen a ghost."

Bingo again, Gwendy thinks, and almost bursts out giggling. "I went for a longer than usual run this morning and haven't had much to drink. I'm probably just dehydrated."

The receptionist gives her a long look, clearly unconvinced. "I'll go grab a couple more waters then. I'll be right back." She turns and heads out of the office.

"Bea?"

She stops in the doorway and turns back.

"Did anyone stop by the office when I was at my meeting this morning?"

Bea shakes her head. "No, ma'am."

"You're certain?"

"Yes, ma'am." She looks around the room. "Is something wrong? Do you need me to call security?"

"No, no," Gwendy says, escorting the older lady the rest of the way out of the room. "But maybe you should call a doctor, since I can't seem to stay awake past lunchtime these days."

Bea once again offers a faint smile, not very convincingly, and hurries off.

Gwendy closes the door and walks a direct line back to the filing cabinet. She knows she doesn't have much time. Bending to a knee again, she slides open the bottom drawer. The button box is still there, practically sparkling in the overhead lights, waiting for her.

Gwendy reaches out with both hands and hesitates, her fingers hovering an inch or two above its highly polished surface. She feels the hairs on her arms begin to tingle, hears the faint whisper of *something* in the far corner of her brain. Steeling herself, she carefully lifts the box out of the drawer. And as she does, it all rushes back to her . . .

10

WHEN GWENDY WAS A young girl, her father hauled the old cardboard box marked SLIDES out of the attic every summer, usually some time around the Fourth of July. He set up his ancient slide projector on the coffee table in the den, positioned the pull-down screen in front of the fireplace, and turned off all the lights. He always made a big deal of the experience. Mom made popcorn and a pitcher of fresh lemonade. Dad narrated every slide with what he called his "Hollywood voice" and made shadow puppets during intermission. Gwendy usually sat on the sofa between her mother and father, but sometimes other neighborhood kids would join them, and on those occasions, she sat on the floor in front of the screen with her friends. Some of the kids grew bored and quickly made up excuses to leave ("Oops, I'm sorry, Mr. Peterson, I just remembered I promised my mom I'd clean my room tonight."), but Gwendy was never one of them. She was fascinated by the images on the screen, and even more so by the stories those images told.

As Gwendy's fingers close around the button box for the first time in fifteen years, it's as if a slideshow of vibrant, flickering images—each one telling its own secret story—blooms in front of her eyes. Suddenly, it's:

—*August 22, 1974, and a strange man in a black coat and a small neat black hat is reaching under a Castle View park bench and sliding out a canvas bag with a drawstring top. He pulls it open and removes the most beautiful mahogany box . . .*

—an early September morning, and Gwendy stands in front of her bedroom closet, dressing for school. When she's finished, she slips a tiny piece of chocolate into her mouth and closes her eyes in ecstasy . . .

—middle school, as Gwendy stares at herself in a full-length dressing room mirror, and realizes she isn't just pretty, she's gorgeous, and no longer wearing eyeglasses . . .

—sophomore year of high school and she's sitting on the den sofa, staring in horror as images of bloated, fly-covered corpses fill the television screen . . .

—late at night, the house graveyard quiet, and she's sitting cross-legged in the dark on her bed with the button box resting in her lap, eyes squeezed tight in concentration, using her thumb to press the red button, and then cocking her head at the open window, listening for the rumble . . .

—a mild spring evening and she's screaming hysterically as two teenaged boys crash into her night table, sending hairbrushes and make-up skittering across the bedroom floor, before reeling into the open closet, falling and pulling down dresses and skirts and pants from their plastic hangers, collapsing to the ground in a heap, and then a filthy hand with blue webbing tattooed across the back of it lifts the button box and brings it crashing down, corner first, into the crown of her boyfriend's skull . . .

Gwendy gasps and she's back in Washington D.C.—and without a moment to spare. She scrambles across her office floor on all fours and vomits into the wastebasket next to her desk.

11

DUE TO THE EXORBITANT cost of maintaining two residences in separate states, many first-year congressional representatives are forced to rent overpriced apartments (a large number of them located in leaky, unventilated basements) or share rented townhouses or condos with multiple roommates. Most do so without complaint. The hours are long, and they rarely find themselves at home anyway except to shower and sleep, or, if they're lucky, eat the occasional unrushed meal.

Gwendy Peterson suffers from no such financial dilemma—thanks to the success of her novels and the resulting movie adaptations—and lives alone in a three-story townhouse located two blocks east of the Capitol Building. Nevertheless, on a near daily basis, she feels no small amount of guilt because of her living situation, and is always quick to offer a spare bedroom should anyone need a place to stay.

Tonight, however, as she sits in the middle of her sofa with her legs curled beneath her, picking at a carton of shrimp lo mein and staring blindly at the television, she is over-the-moon grateful for her solo living arrangements and even more appreciative that she has no overnight guests.

The button box sits on the sofa next to her, looking out of place, almost like a child's toy in the sterile environment of the townhouse. It took Gwendy the better part of the afternoon to figure out how to smuggle the box out of her office. After several failed attempts, she finally settled on dumping her new boots onto the floor of the closet and using the large cardboard box they came in to conceal it under her arm. Fortunately, the security checkpoints set up throughout the building were put in place for arriving personnel only and not for those departing.

A commercial for the new Tom Hanks movie blares on the television, but Gwendy doesn't notice. She hasn't moved from the sofa in the past two hours except to answer the door when the deliveryman rang the bell. Dozens of questions sift through her mind, one after the other in rapid-fire succession, with a dozen more waiting in the shadows to take their place.

Two questions reoccur most frequently as if on a continuous loop:

Why is the box back?
And why now?

12

GWENDY HAS NEVER TOLD a soul about the button box. Not her husband, not her parents, not even Johnathon or the therapist she saw twice a week for six months back in her mid-twenties.

There was a time when the box filled her every waking thought, when she was obsessed with the mystery and the power contained within, but that was a lifetime ago. Now, for the most part, her memories of the box feel like scattered remnants of a recurring dream she once had during childhood, but whose details have long since been lost in the never-ending maze of adulthood. There's a lot of truth to the old adage: out of sight, out of mind.

She has, of course, thought about the box in the fifteen years since it vanished from her life, but—and she's just come to terms with this revelation in the last sixty minutes or so—not nearly as much as she probably should have, considering the immense role the button box played for much of her adolescence.

Looking back, there were weeks, perhaps even months, when it never once crossed her mind and then, boom, she would watch a news report about a mysterious, seemingly natural, disaster that occurred in some faraway state or country, and she would immediately picture someone sitting in a car or at a kitchen table with their finger resting on a shiny red button.

Or she would stumble upon a news teaser online about a man discovering buried treasure in the back yard of his suburban home and would click the link to see if any 1891 Morgan silver dollars were involved.

There were also those dark instances—thankfully rare—when she would catch a glimpse of old grainy video footage on television or hear a snippet of a radio discussion about the Jonestown Massacre in Guyana. When that happened, her heart would skip a beat and set to aching, and she would tumble into a deep black hole of depression for days.

And finally there were those times when she would spot a neat black bowler's hat bobbing up and down amidst a crowd on a busy sidewalk or glance over at an outdoor café table and spy the shiny dome of that black hat resting next to a mug of steaming coffee or a frosty glass of iced tea and, of course, her thoughts would rush back to the man in the black coat. She thought about Richard Farris and that hat of his more than all the rest of it. It was always the mysterious Mr. Farris that swam closest to the surface of her conscious mind. It was his voice she'd heard back in her office, and it is his voice she hears again now, as she sits on the sofa with her bare legs tucked beneath her: *Take care of the box, Gwendy. It gives gifts, but they're small recompense for the responsibility. And be careful . . .*

13

AND WHAT ABOUT THOSE gifts the box so willingly dispenses?

Although she didn't actually witness the narrow wooden shelf slide out from the center of the box with a silver dollar on it, she believes that's where the coin on her desk came from. Coin, box; box, coin; it all made perfect sense.

Does that mean pulling the other lever—*the one on the left side by the red button*, she remembers as if it were yesterday—will deliver a tiny chocolate treat? Maybe. And maybe not. You can never tell with the button box. She believed it had a lot more tricks up its sleeve fifteen years ago, and she believes it even more now.

She brushes her fingertip against the small lever, thinking about the animal-shaped chocolates, no two ever the same, each exotically sweet and no bigger than a jellybean. She remembers the first time she ever laid eyes on one of the chocolates—standing next to Richard Farris in front of the park bench. It was in the shape of a rabbit, and the degree of detail was astounding—the fur, the ears, the cute little eyes! After that, there was a kitty and a squirrel and a giraffe. Her memory grows hazy then, but she remembers enough: eat one chocolate and you were never hungry for seconds; eat a bunch of chocolates over a period of time and you *changed*— you got faster and stronger and smarter. You had more energy and always seemed to be on the winning side of a coin flip or a board game. The chocolates also improved your eyesight and erased your acne. Or had puberty taken care of that last one? Sometimes it was hard to tell.

Gwendy looks down and is horrified to see that her finger has strayed from the small lever on the side of the box to the rows of colored buttons. She jerks her hand back as if it's wrist-deep in a hornet's nest.

But it's too late—and the voice comes again:

"Light green: Asia. Dark green: Africa. Orange: Europe. Yellow: Australia. Blue: North America. Violet: South America."

"And the red one?" Gwendy asks aloud.

"Whatever you want," the voice answers, *"and you* will *want it, the owner of the box always does."*

She gives her head a shake, trying to silence the voice, but it isn't finished yet.

"The buttons are hard to push," Farris tells her. *"You have to use your thumb and put some real muscle into it. Which is a good thing, believe me. Wouldn't want to make any mistakes with those, oh no. Especially not with the black one."*

The black one . . . back then she called it the Cancer Button. She shudders at the memory.

The phone rings.

And for the second time today, Gwendy almost faints.

14

"Ryan! I'm so glad you called."

"I've been trying to get a . . . for days, sweetheart," he says, his voice momentarily gone amidst a blast of static. "Stupid phones here are worthless."

"Here" is the small island of Timor, located off the southern end of Southeast Asia. Ryan's been there since the first week of December with a *Time* magazine crew covering government unrest.

"Are you okay?" Gwendy asks. "Are you safe?"

"I stink like I've been living . . . barn the last couple weeks but I'm fine."

Gwendy laughs. Happy tears stream down her cheeks. She gets up from the sofa and starts pacing back and forth. "Are you going to make it home in time for Christmas?"

"I don't know, honey. I hope so but . . . are heating up here."

"I understand." Gwendy nods her head. "I hope you're wrong, but I understand."

"How's . . . doing?" he says, cutting out again.

"What? I didn't hear you, baby."

"How's your mom doing?"

Gwendy smiles—and then stops in her tracks.

She stares at the curtained window that occupies the upper half of the kitchen door, unsure if it's her imagination. A few seconds pass and she's just about convinced she's seeing things, when a shadow moves again. Someone's outside on the deck.

" . . . hear me?" Ryan says, startling her.

"Oh, she's doing fine," Gwendy says, inching into the kitchen and pulling open a drawer. "Gaining weight and going to her appointments." She takes out a steak knife and holds it against her leg.

"I'll have to make her . . . secret recipe pancakes when I . . . home."

"Just get your butt home in one piece, will you?"

He laughs and starts to say something else, and then there's an ear-piercing jolt of static—and dead air.

"Hello? Hello?" she says, pulling the phone away from her ear so she can look at the screen. "Shit." He's gone.

Gwendy places the cellphone on the counter, crouches, and edges closer to the door. When she reaches the end of the row of cabinets, she crab-walks the last couple of feet into position directly behind the door. Before she can lose her nerve, she lets out a banshee cry and springs to her feet, flipping on the outside light with one hand and using the other hand to flick aside the flowered curtains with the tip of the steak knife.

Whoever was standing outside of the door is gone. All that's left is her wide-eyed reflection staring back at her.

15

THE FIRST THING GWENDY does after retrieving her cellphone from the kitchen counter (even before she walks to the front door and double-checks the deadbolt) is to make sure nothing has happened to the button box. For one terrible, breathless moment, while she's crossing from the kitchen into the family room, she imagines that the figure at the back door was a diversionary tactic, and while she was busy conducting her counterattack, an accomplice was breaking into the front of the house and stealing away with the box.

Her entire body sags with relief when she sees the button box sitting on the sofa right where she'd left it.

A short time later, as she makes her way upstairs carrying the box, it occurs to her that she never once considered telling Ryan about it. At first, she tries to use the severed connection as an excuse, but she knows better. The button box came back to her and only her. Nobody else.

"It's mine," she says as she enters the bedroom.

And shivers at the intensity of her voice.

16

GWENDY SLEEPWALKS HER WAY through December 17, 1999, her final day at the office before Congress begins its three-week holiday break. She spends the first fifteen minutes convincing Bea that she feels well enough to be at work (the day before, the panicked receptionist was ready to call the paramedics when she found Gwendy vomiting into her trash can; luckily, Gwendy was able to convince her that it must've been something bad she ate for breakfast, and after agreeing to go home forty minutes early, the older woman finally relented) and the next eight-and-a-half hours resisting the urge to rush home and check on the button box.

She hated to leave the box back at the townhouse, especially after the scare at her kitchen door the night before, but she didn't have much of a choice. No telling how the X-ray machines at the security checkpoints would react to the box, and perhaps even more worrisome, no telling how the box would react to being X-rayed. Gwendy didn't have a clue what the inside of the button box looked like, or what its innards were made of, but she wasn't taking any chances.

Before she left for her two-block walk to the Capitol Building, she hid the box at the back of a narrow crawlspace underneath the staircase. She stacked cardboard boxes full of books on each side and in front of it, and laid a pile of winter coats on top of it all. Once she was satisfied, she closed the crawlspace's small door, locked up the townhouse, and started for work. She managed only to return home to check on the box twice before finally making it into the office.

Gwendy's last day passes in a blur of faceless voices and background noise. Several phone conferences in the morning and a pair of brief committee meetings in the afternoon. She doesn't remember much of what was said in any of them, or even what she ate for lunch.

When five o'clock rolls around, she locks her office and sets off to deliver Christmas gifts to a handful of co-workers—a set of scented candles and bath salts for Patsy, a cashmere sweater and bracelet for Bea, and a stack of signed books for Bea's children. After well-wishes and hugs goodbye, she heads for the lobby.

17

"I'm sure gonna miss your smiling face these next few weeks, Congresswoman."

"I'm going to miss you, too," Gwendy says, stopping at the security desk. She reaches into her tote bag and pulls out a small box covered in snowman wrapping paper. She hands it across the barrier to the barrel-chested guard. "Merry Christmas, Harold."

Harold's mouth drops open. He slowly reaches out and takes the gift. "You got me . . . this is really for me?"

Gwendy smiles and nods her head. "Of course. I would never forget my favorite head of security."

He looks at her in confusion. "Head of—?" And then he grins and those gold teeth of his wink at her in the fluorescent lights. "Oh, you're joking with me."

"Open your present, silly man."

His meaty fingers attack the wrapping paper and uncover a shiny black box with *Bulova* printed in gold lettering across the top of it. He opens the box and looks up in disbelief. "You bought me a watch?"

"I saw you admiring Congressman Anderson's last week," Gwendy says. "I thought you deserved one of your own."

Harold opens his mouth but no words come out. Gwendy is surprised to see that the guard's eyes have gone shiny and his chin is trembling. "I . . . this is the nicest present anyone has ever given me," he finally says. "Thank you."

For the first time today, Gwendy feels like maybe everything will be okay. "You're very welcome, Harold. I hope you and your family have a wonderful Christmas." She pats his arm affectionately and turns to leave.

"Not so fast," Harold says, raising a hand. He ducks behind the desk and comes back up with a wrapped gift of his own. He hands it to Gwendy.

She looks at him in surprise, and then reads the gift tag: *To Congresswoman Gwendy Peterson; From Harold & Beth.* "Thank you," she says, genuinely touched. "Both of you." She opens the present. It's a thick hardcover book with a bright orange dust jacket. She turns it over so she can see the front cover—and the room shifts, up, down, and up again, like she just sat down on a teeter-totter at the playground.

"You okay, Congresswoman?" Harold asks. "You already have a copy?"

"No, no," Gwendy says, holding up the book. "I've never read it, but I've always wanted to."

"Oh, good," he says, relieved. "I can barely make heads or tails of the jacket copy, but my wife read it and said it was fascinating."

Gwendy forces a smile on her face. "Thank you again, Harold. It really is a lovely surprise."

"Thank *you* again, Congresswoman Peterson. You shouldn't have, but I'm sure glad you did." He bursts out laughing.

Gwendy slips the book inside her leather tote and heads for the elevator. On the ride down, she takes another peek at the cover, just to make sure she's not losing her mind.

She's not.

The book Harold gave her is *Gravity's Rainbow.* It's the same novel Richard Farris was reading on the bench in Castle View twenty-five years earlier—on the day he first gave Gwendy the button box.

18

GWENDY IS LEANING TOWARD canceling her long-scheduled dinner plans with friends even before the copy of *Gravity's Rainbow* shows up, but Harold's well-meaning, yet not-so-pleasant surprise, cinches the deal. She goes straight home, unburies the button box from its hiding place, changes into sweatpants and a baggy sweater, and calls out for delivery.

While her friends—two former classmates from Brown—dine on filet mignon and grilled vegetables at historic Old Ebbitt Grill on Fifteenth (where you have to call weeks in advance for a table), Gwendy sits alone in her dining room, picking at the sorriest excuse for a garden salad she's ever seen and nibbling on a slice of pizza.

She's not really alone, of course. The button box is there, resting on the opposite end of the table, watching her eat like a silent suitor. A few minutes earlier, she looked up from her dinner and asked quite sincerely, "Okay, you're back. What do I do with you now?" The box didn't answer.

Gwendy's attention is currently focused on an evening news program playing on the den television, and she's not happy. She still can't believe Clinton lost to this idiot. "The President of the United States is a flipping moron," she says, stuffing a piece of lettuce that's closer to brown than it is green into her mouth. "You tell 'em, Bernie."

Anchorman Bernard Shaw, with his distinguished salt-and-pepper hair and thick mustache, does just that: ". . . recap the sequence of events that has brought us to this potentially catastrophic standoff. Initially, spy-satellite photographs led U.S. officials to suspect that North Korea was developing a new nuclear facility near the Yongbyon nuclear center that was originally disabled by the 1994 accord. Based on these photographs, Washington demanded an inspection of the facility and Pyongyang countered by demanding the U.S. pay $300 million for the right to inspect the site. Earlier this week, President Hamlin responded angrily—and, many say, disrespectfully—in public comments directed at the North Korean leader, refusing to pay any such inspection fee and calling the proposal 'ludicrous and laughable.' Now, within the past hour, Pyongyang has released a written statement referring to President Hamlin as 'a brainwashed bully' and threatening to pull out of the 1994 accord. No response from the White House yet, but one unnamed official claims . . ."

"That's just great," Gwendy says, getting up from the table and tossing the remains of her salad into the trash. "A pissing contest between two egomaniacs. I'm going to get a lot of calls over this . . ."

19

GWENDY PULLS THE BLANKET over her chest and gives the box one last look before turning off the bedside lamp. Earlier in the evening, after brushing her teeth and washing her face, she placed the button box on the dresser next to her jewelry tray and hairbrushes. Now, she's wondering if she should move it closer. Just to be safe.

She reaches out to turn on the light again—but freezes when she hears the creak of a door opening on hinges that need oiling. She immediately recognizes the sound. It's her closet door.

Unable to move, she watches in terror as a dark figure emerges from inside the walk-in closet. She tries to bark out a warning—*Stop, I have a gun! I'm calling 911!;* anything that might buy her a little more time—but realizes that she's holding her breath. Suddenly remembering the button box on the dresser, she yanks off the thick blanket and scrambles across the bed.

But the intruder is too fast.

He lunges at her, strong arms grabbing her around the waist and wrestling her back onto the bed. She screams and flails at her attacker, clawing at his eyes, ripping off the ski mask he's wearing.

Gwendy sees his face in the glow of the television and gasps.

The intruder is Frankie Stone—somehow alive again

and looking exactly as he did almost twenty years earlier on the night he killed her boyfriend—baggy camo pants, dark glasses, and a tight tee-shirt, wearing that stupid grin of his, greasy brown hair staining his shoulders, shotgun pattern of acne scattered across his cheeks.

He flips her over and pins Gwendy against the mattress, and she can smell the stale, alcohol-tainted foulness of his breath as he hisses, "Give me the box, you dumb bitch. Give it to me right now or I'll eat you alive"—and then his jaws yawn open impossibly wide and the world goes dark as Frankie Stone closes his mouth and engulfs her.

20

GWENDY JERKS UPRIGHT IN bed, clutching a tangle of sweat-soaked sheets to her chest and gasping for breath. Her eyes dart to the closet door across the room—it's closed tight—and then to her dresser. The button box is exactly as she left it, sitting there in the dark with its watchful gaze.

21

"ARE YOU SURE YOU don't want me to stow your bag, Congresswoman Peterson?"

Gwendy looks at the co-pilot who had introduced himself just minutes earlier when she first boarded the eight-seat private plane, but she's already forgotten his name. "No, it's fine. I packed my laptop and I'll probably fiddle around with some work once we're in the air."

"Very well," he says. "We should be taking off in about twenty minutes." He gives her a reassuring smile—the kind that says, *Your life is in my hands, lady, but I slept great last night and only did a little bump of cocaine this morning, so hey it's all good*—and ducks back into the cockpit.

Gwendy yawns and looks out the window at the busy runway. The last thing she wants to do during the short flight is fiddle with her laptop. She's exhausted from not sleeping the night before and in a foul mood. Not even forty-eight hours have passed since the button box's return to her life, and she's already moved on from shock and curiosity to anger and resentment. She glances at her carry-on suitcase, tucked underneath the seat in front of her, and fights the urge to check on the box again.

Squeezing her eyes shut, she tries to silence the obsessive voice chattering away in the back of her head, and abruptly snaps them open again when she realizes she's dozing off.

Sleeping with the box unsecured might not be such a smart idea, she decides.

"Is it safe?" she suddenly asks out loud, without intending to. She looks down at the suitcase again. The flight is less than ninety minutes long. What's the worst that can happen if she takes a little catnap? She doesn't know and she's not willing to find out. She can sleep when she gets home.

Is it safe? She's thinking of the old Dustin Hoffman movie now with the evil Nazi dentist. *Is it safe?*

When it comes to the button box, Gwendy knows the answer to that question. The box is never safe. Not really.

"We're number two for take-off, Congresswoman," the co-pilot says, peeking out from the cockpit. "We should have you on the ground in Castle Rock a few minutes before noon."

22

IF GWENDY'S BEING HONEST with herself—and as the King Air 200 climbs high in the clouds above a muddy twist of Potomac River she's determined to be exactly that—she has to admit that her crummy mood this morning is coming from one overwhelming source: a long-forgotten memory from her youth.

It was a mild and breezy August day shortly before the start of her tenth-grade year in high school, and Gwendy just finished running the Suicide Stairs for the first time in months. When she reached the top, she sat and rested on the same Castle View bench where years earlier she'd first met a man named Richard Farris. She stretched her legs for a moment, and then she leaned her head back and closed her eyes, enjoying the feel of the sun and the wind on her face.

The question that had bloomed in her mind while sitting on the bench that long ago summer day resurfaced—and rather rudely—earlier this morning as Gwendy was busy cushioning the button box in her carry-on bag with rolled up wads of socks and sweaters: *How much of her life is her own doing, and how much the doing of the box with its treats and buttons?*

The memory—and the central thought contained within that memory—was almost enough to make Gwendy scream in rage and fling the box across the bedroom like a toddler in the midst of a temper tantrum.

No matter how she looks at it, Gwendy knows she's led what most people would call a charmed life. There was the scholarship to Brown, the writers' workshop in Iowa, the fast-track job at the ad agency, and of course, the books and movies and Academy Award. And then there was the election, what many pundits called the biggest political upset in Maine history.

Sure, there were failures along the way—a lost advertising account here, a film option that didn't pan out there, and her love life before Ryan could probably best be described as a barren desert of disappointment—but there weren't too many, and she always bounced back with an ease of which others were envious.

Even now, glaring at the button box resting securely between her feet, Gwendy believes with all her heart that the bulk of her success can be attributed to hard work and a positive attitude, not to mention thick skin and persistence.

But what if what she believes to be true . . . simply isn't?

23

A LIGHT SNOW IS falling from a low-hanging, slate gray sky when Gwendy lands at the Castle County Airport out on Route 39. Nothing heavy, just a kiss on the cheek from the north that will leave yards and roadways coated with an inch or so of slush by dinnertime.

She called ahead before boarding the plane and asked Billy Finkelstein, one of only two full-timers at Castle County Airport, to jump her car battery back to life and pull her Subaru hatchback out of one of the three narrow hangars that run alongside the wooded shoulder of Route 39.

Billy is true to his word, and the car's waiting for her in the parking lot, both the engine and heater running hard. She thanks Billy, sliding him a tip even though it's against the rules, and nods hello to his boss, Jessie Martin, one of her father's old bowling partners. She loads her carry-on into the front passenger seat and tosses her tote bag on top of it.

On her way home, Gwendy makes a pair of quick phone calls. The first is to her father to let him know she landed safely and that she'll be there for dinner tonight. Mom's asleep on the sofa, so she doesn't get to speak to her, but Dad's pleased as punch and looking forward to seeing Gwendy later.

The second call is to Castle County Sheriff Norris Ridgewick's cellphone. It rings straight to voicemail, so she leaves a message after the beep: "Hey, Norris, it's Gwendy

Peterson. I just got back into town and figured we ought to touch base. Give me a buzz when you can."

As she presses the END button on her phone, Gwendy feels the Subaru's back tires momentarily loosen their grip on the road. She carefully steers back into the center of the lane and drops her speed. *That's all you need,* she thinks. *Hit a telephone pole, knock yourself unconscious, and have the button box discovered by some nineteen-year-old snowplow driver with a tin of Red Man in his back pocket and frozen snot crusted on his lip.*

24

THERE ARE ONLY TWO ways up to Castle View in 1999: Route 117 and Pleasant Road. Gwendy steers the Subaru onto Pleasant, climbing past a winding half-mile stretch of single homes—ranchers, Cape Cods, and saltbox colonials; many of them decorated for Christmas—and takes a left after the new American Legion playground onto View Drive. She drives another couple hundred yards and then makes a right into the snow-covered parking lot of Castle View Condominiums. Several years ago, she and Ryan were among the first half-dozen folks to purchase a unit in the newly built complex. Despite their busy travel schedules, they've been happy there ever since.

Gwendy swings into a reserved spot in the front row and turns off the engine. Circling to the passenger side to pull out her suitcase, she glances down a series of gently sloping hills to a fenced-off precipice where she once ran a zigzagging metal staircase called the Suicide Stairs. Standing out like a dark scar on the snowy hillside is the wooden bench where she first met the stranger in the black hat.

Gwendy punches in a four-digit security code to gain entrance to her building and climbs the stairs to the second floor. Once inside Unit 19B, she shrugs off her jacket, leaving it on the foyer floor, unzips her suitcase and takes out the button box, carries it down the hallway to the bedroom, places it on her husband's side of the bed, and curls up next to it. Thirty seconds later, she's snoring.

25

GWENDY OPENS HER EYES to the dark silence of her bedroom, disoriented by the lack of daylight at the window, and momentarily forgets where she is. She hustles into the bathroom to pee and experiences a sharp spike of panic in her chest when she remembers dinner with her parents.

After stashing the button box inside a fireproof safe in the office she shares with Ryan, she spends the next five minutes searching for her keys. She finally finds them in the pocket of her jacket on the floor and rushes out the door, determined not to be late.

Driving faster than she should on the slick roads, she's a block away from her parents' house when she thinks about the box again. "It should be safe in the safe," she says out loud and laughs.

The safe was originally her husband's idea. Convinced that they both needed a place to store their valuables, he supervised the purchase and installation of the SentrySafe a few months after they moved into the condo. Of course, several years later, there was nothing inside the thing except for a handful of contracts, old insurance papers, an envelope containing a small amount of cash, and a signed Ted Williams baseball inside a plastic cube—and now the button box.

I can't keep lugging it around with me everywhere I go, Gwendy thinks, turning onto Carbine Street. *Can't keep it in the condo either, not when Ryan gets back.* She'd stored the button box in a safe deposit box at the Bank of Rhode Island during her four years at Brown, and that worked out just fine. Maybe she'd drop by Castle Rock Savings and Loan at the beginning of next week, see what they have available.

Gwendy spots her parents' Cape Cod ahead in the distance and breaks into a smile. Her father has really outdone himself this year. Green and red and blue Christmas bulbs outline the gutters of the roof and spiral up and down the front porch railings. A huge inflatable Santa Claus, illuminated by a series of bright spotlights, dances in the breeze at the center of the front yard. An inflatable red-nosed reindeer grazes in the snow at Santa's feet.

He did all this for Mom, Gwendy realizes, pulling into the driveway and parking behind her father's truck. Still smiling, she gets out and walks to the door. She's home again.

RICHARD CHIZMAR

26

MR. PETERSON IS PREPARING chicken and dumplings for dinner, Gwendy's favorite, and the three of them catch up on everything from the two missing girls to across-the-street neighbor Betty Johnson's sudden conversion to bleach blonde to the New England Patriots three-game losing streak. Mrs. Peterson, looking better than Gwendy has seen her look in months, complains about still needing to take daily naps and her husband's constant coddling, but she does so with a grateful smile and an affectionate squeeze of Mr. Peterson's forearm. She's wearing a different wig tonight—a shade darker and a couple inches longer—than the one she was wearing the last time Gwendy was home, and it not only makes her look healthier, it makes her appear years younger. Her face lights up when Gwendy tells her so.

"Any more news from Ryan?" Mrs. Peterson asks, as her husband gets up and goes into the kitchen to silence the oven timer.

"Not since he called two nights ago," Gwendy says.

"You still think he'll make it home in time for Christmas?"

Gwendy shakes her head. "I don't know, Mom. It all depends on what happens over there. I've been keeping an eye on the news but they haven't reported much yet."

Mr. Peterson walks into the dining room carrying a plate stacked high with biscuits. "Saw President Hamlin on the tube earlier this evening. I still can't believe our Gwendy gets to work with the Commander-in-Chief."

Mrs. Peterson gives her daughter a smile and rolls her eyes. She's heard this spiel before. Many times. They both have.

"Have you spoken with him lately?" he asks eagerly.

"A bunch of us were in a meeting with him and the vice president last week," Gwendy says.

Her father beams with pride.

"Trust me, it's not all that it's cracked up to be."

As is often the case, she's tempted to tell her father the reality of the situation: that President Hamlin is a sexist bore of a man who rarely looks Gwendy in the eyes, instead focusing on her legs if she's wearing a dress or her chest if she's wearing pants; that she purposely never stands too close to the Commander-in-Chief because of his tendency to touch her on the arms and shoulders when he speaks to her. She's also tempted to tell him that the President's as dumb as a donut and has horrible breath, but she doesn't say any of these things. Not to her father, anyway. Now her mother is a different story.

"I liked what he said about North Korea," Mr. Peterson says. "We need a strong leader to deal with that madman."

"He's acting more like a petulant child right now than a leader."

Her father gives her a thoughtful look. "You really don't like him, do you?"

"It's not that . . ." she says. *Careful, girl.* "I just don't care for his policies. He's cut healthcare funds for the poor every year he's been in office. He cut federal funding for AIDS clinics and reinforced anti-gay legislation across the board. He spearheaded a movement to reduce budgets for the arts in public schools. I just wish he cared more about people and less about winning every argument."

63

Her father doesn't say anything.

Gwendy shrugs. "What can I say? He's just a muggle, Dad."

"What's a muggle?" he asks.

Mrs. Peterson touches his arm. "From Harry Potter, dear."

He looks around the table. "Harry who?"

This time his wife smacks him on the arm. "Oh, stop it, you smart aleck."

They all crack up laughing.

"Had you going for a minute," he says, winking.

For the next several hours, Gwendy relaxes and the button box hardly crosses her mind. There's one brief moment, when she's standing at the kitchen window overlooking the back yard, and she spots the old oak tree towering in the distance and remembers once hiding the box in a small crevice at the base of its thick trunk. But the memory's gone from her head as quickly as it arrives, and within seconds, she's back in the den watching *Miracle on 34th Street* and working on a crossword puzzle with her father.

27

". . . INITIALLY OCCURRED WHEN ANTI-INDEPENDENCE militants launched an attack on a crowd of unarmed civilians."

An expression of grim sincerity is etched on the Channel Five newscaster's face, as a banner headline reading BREAKING NEWS: CRISIS IN TIMOR scrolls across the bottom of the screen. "There are early reports of violence and bloodshed spreading throughout the countryside, the worst of the fighting centered in the capital city of Dili. The fighting erupted after a majority of the island's eligible voters chose independence from Indonesia. Over two hundred civilian casualties have already been reported with that number expected to rise."

Gwendy sits at the foot of the bed, dressed in a long flannel nightgown, the button box propped up on a pillow beside her, its twin rows of multi-colored buttons looking like teeth in the glow of the television.

The anchorman promises more breaking news from Timor just as soon as it becomes available, and then Channel Five goes to commercial.

At first, Gwendy doesn't move, doesn't even seem to breathe, and then she turns to the box and in an odd, toneless voice says, "Curiosity killed the cat." She uses her pinky to pull the lever on the right side of the box.

A narrow wooden shelf slides out from the center with a silver dollar on it. Gwendy picks up the shiny coin and, without looking at it, places it beside her on the bed. The shelf slides back in without a sound.

"But satisfaction brought it back," she recites in that same odd voice and pulls the other lever.

The wooden tray slides out again, this time dispensing a tiny piece of chocolate in the shape of a horse.

She picks up the chocolate with two steady fingers and looks at it with amazed wonder. Lifting it to her face, she closes her eyes and breathes in the sweet, otherworldly aroma. Her eyes open lazily and gaze at the chocolate with a look of naked desire. She licks her lips as they begin to part—

—and then she's fleeing to the bathroom, hot tears streaming from her eyes, and flushing the chocolate horse down the toilet.

28

THE FIRST PERSON GWENDY sees when she walks into the Castle Rock Diner on Sunday morning is Old Man Pilkey, the town's retired postmaster. Hank Pilkey is going on ninety years old and has a glass left eye as the result of a fly-fishing accident. Rumor has it his second wife, Ruth, got drunk on moonshine and caused the injury while they were honeymooning in Nova Scotia. When Gwendy was young, she was terrified of the old man and dreaded tagging along with her parents to the post office on Saturday mornings. It wasn't that she was spooked or even grossed out by the shiny prosthetic eyeball. She was simply a nervous wreck that she'd go into some kind of weird staring trance and cause the old guy discomfort or, even worse, embarrassment.

Fortunately, years of practice have helped to ease Gwendy's fears, and when she swings open the diner's front door—a pair of HAVE YOU SEEN THIS GIRL? posters taped to the outside of the thick glass—at a few minutes before ten and Old Man Pilkey spots her with a toothless grin, hops down from his stool in front of the long Formica counter and opens his saggy arms in greeting, Gwendy looks him in the eye and hugs him back with genuine affection.

"There's our hometown hero," he croaks, gripping her shoulders with bony fingers and holding her at arm's length so he can get a good look at her.

Gwendy laughs and it feels good after the long night she's just had. "How are you, Mr. Pilkey?"

"Fair to middling," he says, easing back onto the stool. "Fair to middling."

"And how's Mrs. Pilkey?"

"Ornery as ever, and twice as sweet."

"Fair words to describe the both of you," Gwendy says and gives him a wink. "Enjoy your Sunday, Mr. Pilkey."

"You do the same, young lady. My best to your folks."

Gwendy walks to an empty table by the window, nodding hello to several other townspeople, many of them dressed in church clothes, and sits down. Gazing around the diner, she estimates she knows two-thirds of the people in there. Maybe more. She also estimates that maybe half of them voted for her last November. Castle Rock's her hometown, but it's still—and probably always will be—a Republican hotspot.

"I thought that was you."

Gwendy looks up, startled.

"Jesus, Norris. You scared me."

"Sorry about that," he says. "Whole damn town's on edge." He gestures to the empty chair. "Mind if I sit?"

"Please," Gwendy says.

The sheriff sits down and adjusts his gun belt on his hip. "I got your message. Was planning to call you back this morning, but I needed coffee first. Late night."

Norris Ridgewick is two years older than Gwendy and has occupied the Castle County Sheriff's Office since taking over for Alan Pangborn in late 1991. Standing a hint over five-foot-six and weighing in at an even one hundred and fifty pounds (wearing his uniform, shoes, and sidearm), the sheriff doesn't make much of a physical impression, but he more than makes up for it by being resourceful and kind.

Gwendy has always believed that Norris carries a deep well of sadness within him—most likely due to losing his father when he was just fourteen years old and his mother a decade later. Gwendy likes him a lot.

"Why so late?" she asks. "Anything new with the girls?"

The sheriff's eyes wander around the diner. Gwendy follows his gaze and notices many of the other diners have stopped eating and are staring at them. "Not much," he says, lowering his voice. "We're checking out some leads with the Tomlinson girl. A part-time teacher at her school. A custodian at the dance studio she attended. But neither are exactly what I'd call . . . prime suspects."

"And the Hoffman girl?"

He shrugs and waves to get a waitress's attention. "That one's even tougher. We've got the timeframe down to just under fourteen minutes. That's how long the brother was out of the house. In those fourteen minutes, someone smashed the glass on the back door, entered the house, took Carla Hoffman from her bedroom, and disappeared without a trace."

"Without a trace," Gwendy repeats in a whisper.

He nods. "Or much of a struggle, evidently. No prints on the door or anywhere inside the house. It'd snowed that morning but the kids had a snowball fight in the yard, so it was a mess. No chance of boot- or footprints. Could've come by car, but none of the neighbors saw or heard anything."

"Anything coming in on the tip-line?" she asks. "I saw the Hoffmans put up a reward."

"Bunch of calls . . . but only a handful worth following up on, which we're doing."

"Nothing else?"

The sheriff shrugs. "We're trying our damnedest to find

a connection between the two girls, but so far it's not there. They live in different neighborhoods, attend different schools, have different hair color, body types, hobbies. No sign that they knew each other or had close mutual friends. Neither has a boyfriend or has ever been in any kind of trouble."

"What are the chances the two disappearances aren't related?"

"Doubtful."

"What's your gut say?"

"My gut says I need coffee." He glances around for the waitress again.

Gwendy gives him an irritated look.

"What?" he asks. "You believe in all that gut instinct mumbo jumbo?"

"I do," she says.

The sheriff pulls in a deep breath, lets it out. He glances out the window before meeting Gwendy's eyes again. "Lotta weird shit has happened in the Rock over the years, you know that. The Big Fire in '91, boogeyman Frank Dodd murdering those folks, Sheriff Bannerman and those other men getting killed by that rabid Saint Bernard, hell, even the Suicide Stairs. You believe it was an earthquake that knocked them down, I got a bridge to sell you."

Gwendy sits there and offers up her best poker face, an expression she's nearly perfected after less than a year in Washington D.C.

"I hope to hell I'm wrong," he says, sighing heavily, "but I have a feeling we're never gonna see those girls again. Not alive anyway."

29

AFTER BREAKFAST, GWENDY STROLLS across the street to the Book Nook and picks up the Sunday editions of both *The New York Times* and *The Washington Post*. The owner of the bookstore, a stylish woman in her mid-fifties named Grace Featherstone, greets her with a hug and several minutes of colorfully worded grievances relating to President Hamlin. Gwendy stands at the counter, unable to get a word in, nodding enthusiastically. When the older woman finally takes a breath, Gwendy pays for the newspapers and a pack of mints. Then she goes outside and sits in her car, scanning both publications for news about Timor, or more importantly, photographs from Timor.

Several years earlier, Ryan was sent to Brazil to help cover a story about a number of seaside villages that had been taken over and eventually destroyed by a local drug lord. He spent three weeks hiding in the jungle with armed guerillas, unable to contact home in any fashion. During this time, the only way Gwendy was able to confirm Ryan's safety was by locating his photo credits in the daily newspapers and a handful of websites on the Internet. Ever since, in similarly trying times, this method became Gwendy's safety net of last resort. Just seeing Ryan's name printed in tiny type next to one of his photographs was enough to calm her heart for the next day or two until the next photo made an appearance.

Gwendy checks and double-checks both papers—her

fingertips growing dark with smudged ink, the passenger seat and dashboard disappearing beneath a mountain of loose pages and advertising circulars—but doesn't find any photographs. Each newspaper carries a brief article, but they're buried on inside pages and are mostly rehashes of old stories. The Associated Press recently reported online that a United Nations force consisting of mainly Australian Defense Force personnel was deployed to East Timor to establish and maintain peace. After that, not much else was known.

30

Gwendy spends the majority of Sunday afternoon Christmas shopping with her mom. Their first stop is the Walmart, where Gwendy picks up a couple of jigsaw puzzles for her father and Mrs. Peterson snatches the last remaining Sony Walkman on the shelf for Blanche Goff, her longtime neighbor and friend "to use on her morning strolls around the high school track."

Gwendy's cellphone rings as they're walking to the parking lot. It's her father checking in to see how Mom is faring. Gwendy gives her mother a look and tells him everything's fine and promises to keep an eye on her. Before she hangs up, Mrs. Peterson grabs the phone from her daughter's hand and says, "Just watch your football games and leave us alone, you old nag." The two of them climb into the Subaru, stashing their bags in the back seat and giggling like a couple of teenagers.

The truth is Gwendy *has* been keeping close tabs on her mother, and so far she's delighted with what she's seen. Mrs. Peterson is still a bit frail and she's definitely slower on her feet, but all that's to be expected after everything she's been through. More important, to Gwendy at least, is the fact that her mother's cheery attitude and whip-smart sense of humor are back, not to mention that sweet smile of hers. There'd been barely a glimpse of those things during the eight weeks of chemotherapy.

After Walmart, the two women grab a light lunch at Cracker Barrel and head to the mall out on Route 119. The two-story shopping mall is as crowded and noisy as a Friday night football game—it seems like half of Castle Rock's teenage population is there that afternoon—but they don't let it take away from their fun. Gwendy and her mom spend the next couple hours knocking off the final items on their gift lists, eating double-scoop ice cream cones while people-watching in the food court, and singing along to the never-ending selection of Christmas carols playing over the mall's sound system.

At their final stop of the day, Gwendy leaves her mom sitting on a bench outside of Bart's Sporting Goods, and goes inside to purchase a rain-suit for Ryan to wear kayaking. It was his only gift request before he left, and she's determined to have it waiting for him under the tree. Gwendy is stuffing the credit card receipt into her bag and not looking where she's going when she bumps into another shopper on her way out of the store.

"I am so sorry," Gwendy says and then looks up and sees who it is. "Oh my God, Brigette!"

The tall, blonde woman laughs and picks up the shopping bag that was jostled from her hand. "Same old Gwendy, always running somewhere."

Brigette Desjardin was two years ahead of Gwendy at Castle Rock High. Back in those days, they ran indoor track together and spent a lot of time at each other's houses.

"I haven't seen you since what . . . the Fourth of July parade?" Gwendy asks, giving her friend a hug.

"You ran into me that day, too."

Gwendy covers her mouth. "Oh my God, you're right, I did. I am so sorry." Gwendy had knocked a glass of lemonade right out of Brigette's hand and all over her brand-new sundress. "I never used to be so darn clumsy, but I think I'm making up for lost time these past few years."

"That's okay, Gwen," says Brigette, laughing. "I think I know a way you can make it up to me."

"Tell me."

Brigette raises her eyebrows. "Well, you probably haven't heard, but I was elected president of the PTA in September."

"That's terrific," Gwendy says with sincere admiration. "Congratulations."

"Oh, whatever." Brigette rolls her eyes and smiles. "Miss Big-Shot Senator."

"I'm not a—"

"Anyhoo, I'm in charge of the New Year's Eve celebration this year—weather permitting, we're holding it outside in the Common—and I was wondering . . ."

Gwendy doesn't say anything. She can guess what's coming next.

". . . if you might stop by and say a few words?"

One of her mother's favorite sayings flits through her mind: *Don't choose the easy thing to do, choose the* right *thing to do.*

"It would only be for three or four minutes, but I understand if you can't or don't want to or you already have other—"

Gwendy places a hand on her old friend's shoulder. "I'd be happy to."

Brigette squeals and throws her arms around Gwendy. "Thank you, thank you! You have no idea what this means to me."

"Just make sure you're not holding a mug of hot chocolate when you see me coming."

Brigette giggles, relaxing her bear hug. "Deal."

"I'll give you a call next week so you can tell me when and where to show up."

"Perfect. Thank you again *so* much." She starts walking away, and then turns back. "A very merry Christmas to you and your family."

"Merry Christmas. I'm glad I ran into you."

Gwendy turns and starts wading through the crowded promenade. Halfway to the bench where she'd left her mom, Mrs. Peterson comes into view and Gwendy raises a hand to wave—but she never gets that far.

Her mother isn't alone.

A stab of terror piercing her chest, Gwendy starts pushing her way through the crowd.

31

"WHO WAS THAT?" GWENDY nearly shouts, frantically scanning the throng of shoppers behind the bench. "Who were you just talking to?"

Mrs. Peterson looks up in surprise. "What . . . what's wrong?"

"The man with the black hat, the one you were just talking to . . . did you know him?"

"No. He said he's visiting with friends in town. He asked me a couple of questions and went on his way."

"What friends?"

"I didn't ask him that," Mrs. Peterson says. "What's going on, Gwen?"

Up on her tip-toes now, still searching the crowd. "What kind of questions did he ask?"

"Well, let me think . . . he asked how I liked it here in Castle Rock. I told him I'd lived here my entire life, that it was home."

"What else?"

"He wanted to know if I could recommend a good restaurant for dinner. He said he hadn't had a decent hot meal in weeks and was very hungry, which I thought was rather odd considering how nicely he was dressed."

"What else?"

"That was it. It was a very brief conversation."

"What did he look like? Can you describe him?"

"He was . . ." She thinks for a moment. "Tall and thin and probably about your age. I think he had blue eyes."

Mrs. Peterson stands and picks up her shopping bags from the bench. "Now are you going to tell me what's going on, or do I have to start worrying about you, too?"

Thinking fast, Gwendy looks at her mom with that same blank poker face. "There's a reporter who's been bothering me these past few weeks. He's persistent and not a very nice man. For a minute, I was afraid he followed me all the way up here from DC."

"Oh, dear," Mrs. Peterson says, and Gwendy immediately feels horrible for lying to her. "This gentleman seemed very kind, but I guess you can never really tell, can you?"

Gwendy gives her a quick nod. "It's getting harder and harder, that's for sure."

32

THE COLD AIR FEELS good in Gwendy's lungs and the burn in her legs is like catching up with an old friend. After dropping off her mom at the house, she wanted nothing more than to drive home to the condo and head straight upstairs to bed, but her brain had other ideas. Especially after the scare she experienced at the mall.

She follows Pleasant Road down the winding hill, the street well lit and cheery with yard after yard of twinkling Christmas lights, until it runs into Route 117. The road grows darker here, just the occasional pole lamp casting dim globes of sickly yellow light onto the ground below, and she picks up her pace, heading for the old covered bridge that stretches across the Bowie Stream.

Running is usually just as much an act of meditation for Gwendy as it is a form of exercise. On those rare bad weather days when she's forced to work out on the treadmill or StairMaster at the YMCA, she often listens to music on her Sony Walkman—usually something upbeat and peppy like Britney Spears or the Backstreet Boys; a fact Ryan never fails to give her grief about—but during her outside jaunts, she almost always prefers to run in silence. Just her and her inner-most thoughts, the familiar sounds of the city or the country-side, and the rhythmic slap of her shoes punishing the asphalt.

Tonight she's thinking about her husband.

Of course, she's worried about him and anxious he won't

make it home in time for Christmas, but she knows those concerns are out of her control and even a little bit selfish. Ryan has a job to do, a sometimes dangerous job he loves with all his heart, and she supports that passion unconditionally—as he does hers. It's part of what makes them work so well together. On a daily basis, they may prefer the simplicity of each other's company—a walk in the woods, a game of gin rummy at the kitchen table, a late night double-feature at the drive-in—to crowded black tie events and fancy art openings, but when work calls they each know the drill. True passion is almost always accompanied by sacrifice.

So why all the angst this time? Gwendy wonders, as she approaches the old bridge. It's not like this is their first rodeo. Ryan's gone away on dozens of other assignments since they've been together.

A steady stream of likely answers trickles through her mind as she runs: it's because of the holidays; it's because her mother is still recovering from a life-altering illness; it's because the button box is back in her life and she doesn't have a clue what to do with it.

Gwendy considers the question a little longer, then checks off All Of The Above and picks up her stride, focusing on the road ahead.

The streetlight attached to the covered bridge's outer planking is dark, most likely having served as target practice for some bored townie with a .22 rifle. The entrance looms ahead like a dark, hungry mouth, but Gwendy doesn't break pace. She glides into the heart of the pitch-dark tunnel, rapid footsteps echoing around her, reminding her, just as they did when she was a little girl, of the old fairy tale about the evil troll living under the bridge.

It's just a story, she tells herself, pumping her arms.

Nothing's going to reach out and grab you. Nothing's going to leap down from the rafters and—

She's a few yards away from reaching the exit when she hears a noise in the darkness behind her. A furtive scratching like claws scrambling across pavement. A finger of dread tickles the length of her spine. She doesn't want to turn and look, but she can't help herself. A pair of close-set eyes, unblinking and coal-red, watches her from deep within the shadows. Gwendy feels her legs begin to falter and wills them to keep moving, her breath coming fast and ragged. By the time she looks away, she's clear of the bridge and back under the stars on Route 117.

Probably just a stupid raccoon, Gwendy thinks, sidestepping around a pothole in the road. Pulling cool air deeply into her lungs, she keeps running, a little faster now, and doesn't look back.

33

WITH ALL OF HER Christmas shopping completed and the bulk of her work correspondence caught up, Gwendy spends the Monday and Tuesday before Christmas settling into an almost scandalously lazy routine. For her, anyway.

On Monday morning, she sleeps in (waking almost ninety minutes later than her usual 6:00 AM, having forced herself not to set her alarm the night before) and remains in bed until nearly noon, catching up on news programs and movies on cable. After a luxuriously long bubble bath, she makes a light lunch and retires to the sunroom, where she stretches out on the loveseat and alternates between staring out the floor-to-ceiling windows and daydreaming, and reading the new Ridley Pearson thriller deep into the afternoon. Once the December sun begins its inevitable slide toward the horizon, she marks her page, leaves the thick paperback on an end table, and goes upstairs to change clothes. Then she grabs her keys and heads to her parents' house for dinner.

After nearly three months of being waited on in her own kitchen, Mrs. Peterson is finally feeling strong enough to cook again. Under the watchful eye of her husband, Mrs. Peterson prepares and serves a steaming hot casserole of beef stroganoff and a Christmas tree-shaped platter stacked with homemade rolls. The food is delicious, and Mrs. Peterson is so openly and endearingly pleased with herself, her smiles bring tears to her husband's eyes.

After dinner, Gwendy and her father shoo Mrs. Peterson into the den while they clear the table and wash the dishes. Then they join her in watching *A Christmas Carol* on television and crack open a new jigsaw puzzle.

At a few minutes before nine, Gwendy bids her folks goodnight and drives back to the condo. She considers going for a run, but decides against it, working the three-digit combination on the safe instead, and taking out the button box.

It keeps her company at the foot of the bed while she changes into a nightgown and brushes her teeth. She finds herself talking to it more and more now, just as she did when she was younger. The box doesn't answer, of course, but she's almost certain that it listens—and watches. Before she puts it away for the night, she sits on the edge of the mattress, places the box in her lap, and pulls the lever by the red button. The narrow shelf slides out and on it is a tiny chocolate monkey. She admires the fine detail, and then slowly lifts it to her nose and inhales. Her eyes flutter closed. When she opens them again, she gets up and walks at a deliberate pace to the bathroom where she flushes the chocolate down the toilet. Unlike last time, there is no panic and there are no tears. "See?" she says to the box as she reenters the bedroom, "I'm in control here. Not you." And then she returns the button box to the safe and goes to sleep.

Tuesday is more or less a repeat performance of the day before, and there are moments when Gwendy can't help but think of scenes from *Groundhog Day*, that silly movie Ryan likes so much.

She starts the day by again sleeping in and lounging in bed for most of the morning. Then she takes a long bath, finishes the Pearson novel shortly after lunch, and devours the first four chapters of a new John Grisham.

She's not in much of a holiday mood, but she forces herself to haul out the artificial tree and boxes of ornaments from the crawlspace. She sets up the tree in the corner of the family room and hangs last year's wreath on the front door. When dusk descends upon Castle Rock, she goes upstairs to change and heads to her parents' for another dose of Mom's home cooking. Lasagna and salad are on the menu tonight, and Gwendy eats two generous servings of each. After dinner, she and her father once again take care of the dishes, and then join Mrs. Peterson in the den. Tonight's feature is *White Christmas*, and when the movie's over and the credits are rolling, Mr. Peterson shocks both his wife and daughter by rolling up his pant legs, doing his best Bing Crosby imitation, and performing the "Sisters" routine in its entirety. Mrs. Peterson, hardly believing her eyes, collapses onto the sofa laughing so hard she ends up having a coughing fit, prompting her husband to hightail it into the kitchen for a glass of cold water. She takes a big drink, starts hiccupping, and lets out a tremendous belch—and the three of them burst out in delirious laughter all over again. The party breaks up a short time later, and Gwendy heads home, snow flurries dancing in the beams of her car's headlights.

She takes her time driving across town and walks into her condo at precisely nine-thirty, juggling and almost dropping the stack of Tupperware containers her mom sent home with her. There's enough leftover lasagna, stroganoff, and cheesecake in there to last well into the New Year. She's struggling to open the refrigerator when her cellphone rings. Gwendy glances at the counter where she left the phone next to her keys and turns her attention back to the refrigerator. She slides the largest container onto the top shelf next to half-empty cartons of milk and orange juice,

RICHARD CHIZMAR

and is trying to make room on a lower shelf when the phone rings again. She ignores it and jams in the other two containers, one after the other. The phone rings a third time as Gwendy is closing the refrigerator door, and it's almost as if a lightning bolt reaches down from the heavens and strikes some sense into her.

She lunges for the cellphone, knocking her keys onto the floor.

"Hello? Hello?"

At first there's nothing—and then a burst of loud static.

"Hello?" she says again, disappointment washing over her. "Is anyone—"

"Hey, baby girl . . . I was just about to hang up."

Every muscle in her body goes limp, and she has to lean against the table to keep from falling. "Ryan . . ." she says, but it comes out in a whisper.

"You there, Gwen?"

"I'm here, honey. I'm so happy to hear your voice." The tears come now, gushing down her face.

"Listen . . . I don't know how long this line's gonna last. We haven't even been able to file our reports with the magazine or any of the newspapers . . . yesterday . . . fires all over the place."

"Are you okay, Ryan? Are you safe?"

"I'm okay. I wanted to tell you . . . taking care of myself and doing my best . . . get home to you."

"I miss you so damn much," she says, unable to keep the emotion from her voice.

"I miss you, too, baby . . . know when I'll be able to call again, but I'll keep trying . . . by Christmas."

"You're breaking up."

Staccato bursts of static hijack the line. Gwendy pulls the phone away from her ear and waits for them to decrease in intensity. Amidst the noise, she hears her husband's faint voice: ". . . love you."

She presses the phone back to her ear. "Hello? Are you still there? Please take care of yourself, Ryan!" She's nearly shouting now.

The line crackles and then goes silent. She holds it tight against her ear, listening and hoping for one more word—anything—but it doesn't come.

"I love you more," she finally whispers, and ends the call.

34

FORTY-EIGHT HOURS OF LAZINESS (she tries to tell herself she wasn't actually being lazy, she was simply relaxing and decompressing—but she's not buying it) is all Gwendy can tolerate. On Wednesday, she wakes up at dawn and goes for a run.

A sleety, granular snow is falling and the roads are slick with ice, but Gwendy pushes forward, the hood of her sweatshirt cinched tight around her face. Running through downtown Castle Rock is usually a comforting experience for Gwendy. She jogs her normal route—down Main Street, avoiding the unshoveled sidewalks, past the Common, the library, and the Western Auto, circling the long way around the hospital and heading uptown past the Knights of Columbus hall and back toward View Drive—and she feels a sense of rightness in her world, a sense of *belonging*. She's traveled all over the country for her work—first as an ad exec, then as a writer/filmmaker, and finally as a public servant—but there's only one Castle Rock, Maine. Just as her mother had told the stranger in the black hat at the mall, this is home.

But something feels off today.

This morning she feels like a visitor traveling through a foreign and unfriendly landscape. Her mind is cluttered and distracted, her legs sluggish and heavy.

At first she blames this feeling on the way her phone call

with Ryan ended the night before—so abrupt and unsettled. After hanging up, she cried herself to sleep with worry.

But when she passes in front of the sheriff's station as she makes her way uptown, she realizes it's something else entirely. For the first time, she understands how much she's dreading the difficult task that awaits her later that morning.

35

GWENDY'S FIRST IMPRESSION OF Caroline Hoffman is that she's a woman who is used to getting her own way.

When Gwendy walks into the stationhouse at 9:50 AM (a full ten minutes early for the meeting), she's hoping the Hoffmans haven't arrived yet so she and Sheriff Ridgewick will have time to discuss the investigation.

Instead, the three of them are waiting for her in the conference room. There's no sign of Sheila Brigham, the longtime dispatcher for the Castle Rock Sheriff's Department, so Deputy George Footman escorts Gwendy inside and closes the door behind her.

Sheriff Ridgewick sits on one side of a long, narrow table, a chair standing empty next to him. Mr. and Mrs. Hoffman sit side-by-side across from him, a second empty chair separating them. They make an interesting couple. Frank Hoffman is slight in stature, bespectacled, and dressed in a wrinkled brown suit that has seen better days. He has dark circles under his eyes and a slender nose that has been broken more than once. Caroline Hoffman is at least three or four inches taller than her husband, and thick and broad across the shoulders and chest. She could be a female lumberjack, something not unheard of in this part of the world. She's wearing jeans and a gray Harley Davidson sweatshirt with the sleeves rolled up. A tattoo of a boat anchor decorates one meaty forearm.

"Sorry to keep you waiting," Gwendy says, taking a seat beside the sheriff. She places her leather tote on the table in front of her, but quickly removes it and puts it on the floor when she realizes it's dripping wet from melting snow. She uses the sleeve of her sweater to wipe up the small puddle left behind.

"Morning, Congresswoman," Sheriff Ridgewick says.

"Can we get started now?" Mrs. Hoffman asks, glaring at the sheriff.

"Sure thing."

Gwendy leans forward and extends her hand, first to Mr. Hoffman and then to his wife. "Good morning, I'm Gwendy Peterson. I'm very sorry to meet you both under these circumstances."

"Good morning," Mr. Hoffman says in a surprisingly deep voice.

"We know who you are," Mrs. Hoffman says, wiping her hand on her pant leg, like she touched something unsavory. "Question is, how you gonna help us?"

"Well," Gwendy says, "I'll do whatever I can to help locate your daughter, Mrs. Hoffman. If Sheriff Ridgewick needs—"

"Her name is Carla," the big woman interrupts, eyes narrowing again. "Least you can do is say her damn name."

"Of course. I'll do whatever I can to help find Carla. If the sheriff needs additional personnel, I'll make sure he has it. If he needs more equipment or vehicles, I'll make sure he has that, too. Whatever it takes."

Mrs. Hoffman looks at Sheriff Ridgewick. "What the sheriff needs is someone to come in here and show him how to do his job properly."

Gwendy bristles. "Now wait a minute, Mrs. Hoffman—"

91

The sheriff touches Gwendy's forearm, silencing her. He looks at the Hoffmans. "I know you folks are desperate for answers. I know you're unhappy with the way the investigation is progressing."

Mrs. Hoffman snickers. "Progressing."

"But I assure you me and my men are working around the clock to chase down every single scrap of possible evidence. No one will rest until we find out what happened to your daughter."

"We're just so worried," Mr. Hoffman says. "We're both sick with worry."

"I understand that," the sheriff says. "We all do."

"Jenny Tucker over the hair salon says your guys were checking out the Henderson farm yesterday," Mrs. Hoffman says. "Wanna tell me why that is?"

The sheriff sighs and shakes his head. "Jenny Tucker's the biggest gossip in town. You know that."

"Doesn't make it not true."

"No, it doesn't. But in this case it's *not* true. Far as I know, no one's been out to the Henderson place."

"Why not?" she presses. "From what I hear he did time in Shawshank when he was younger."

"Hell, Mrs. Hoffman, half the hard-grit laborers in Castle County served time at one point or another. We can't go searching all their houses."

"Tell us this," she says, cocking her head to the side like an agitated rooster. "And give us a straight answer for a change. What *do* you have? After a full week of walking around in circles, what *do* you have?"

Sheriff Ridgewick lets out a deep breath. "We've talked about this before. I can't tell you anything more than I already have. In order to protect the integrity of the investigation—"

Mrs. Hoffman slams a heavy fist down on the table, startling everyone in the room. "Bullshit!"

"Caroline," Mr. Hoffman says, "maybe we should—"

Mrs. Hoffman turns on her husband, eyes burning. The thick veins in her neck look like they're going to explode. "They got nuthin', Frank. Just like I told ya. They ain't got a goddamn thing."

Gwendy has been listening to all of this with a sense of disconnected awe, almost as though she were sitting in the front row of a studio audience at an afternoon talk show—but something inside her awakens now. She raises a hand in an effort to take control of the room and says, "Why don't we all just take a minute and start over again?"

Glaring at Gwendy, Mrs. Hoffman suddenly jerks to her feet, knocking over her chair. "Why don't ya save that happy horseshit for the folks 'round here who were dumb enough to vote for ya?" She kicks the chair out from under her feet, spittle spraying from the corners of her mouth. "Coming in here with your fancy clothes and five-hundred-dollar boots, trying to shine us on like we're stupid or somethin'!" Flinging open the door, she storms out.

Gwendy stares after Mrs. Hoffman with her mouth hanging open. "I didn't mean to . . . I was just trying . . ."

Mr. Hoffman stands. "Congresswoman, sheriff, you'll have to excuse my wife. She's very upset."

"It's no problem at all," Sheriff Ridgewick says, escorting him to the door. "We understand."

"I apologize if anything I said made matters worse," Gwendy says.

Mr. Hoffman shakes his head. "Things can't get much worse, ma'am." He looks closely at Gwendy. "Do you have children of your own, Congresswoman?"

Gwendy tries to swallow the lump that rises in her throat. "No. I don't."

Mr. Hoffman looks down at the ground and nods, but he doesn't say anything further. Then he shuffles out of the room.

Sheriff Ridgewick stares after him and turns back to Gwendy. "That went well."

Gwendy looks around the conference room, unsure of what to do next. It all happened so fast her head is swirling. She finally blurts out, "I bought these boots at Target."

36

GWENDY MOPES AROUND THE condo for the rest of the afternoon, watching cable news and drinking too much coffee.
She left the sheriff's office hours earlier feeling depressed
and incompetent in equal measures, like she let everyone
in the room down. She obviously said something to stoke
Mrs. Hoffman's ire, and the sheriff was doing just fine handling the two of them before she went and opened her big
mouth. And that smartass comment about her clothes and
boots . . . it bothered Gwendy. It shouldn't have, she knows
that, but it did. Since returning to Castle Rock after all
those years away, she'd grown used to the occasional snide
dig. It came with the territory. So why did she let it get to
her like that?

"Well, don't just sit there," she says to the button box.
"Figure it out and get back to me."

The box ignores her. It sits there—on the end table, next
to a half-empty mug of coffee and an outdated *TV Guide*—
and answers her with stubborn silence. She grabs the remote
and turns up the volume on the television.

President Hamlin stands at the edge of the White House
lawn, his arms crossed in defiance, the Marine One helicop-
ter whirring in the background. ". . . and if they continue to
make these threats against the United States of America," he
says, flashing his best tough-guy look at the camera, "we will

95

have no alternative but to fight power with power. This great country will not back down."

Gwendy watches in disbelief. "Jesus, he thinks he's in a movie."

Her cellphone rings. She knows it's too soon to hear from Ryan again, but she scrambles across the sofa and snatches it up anyway. "Hello?"

"Hey, Gwen. It's Dad."

"I was just thinking about you guys," she says, muting the television. "Need me to bring anything for dinner?"

There's a slight pause before he answers. "That's why I'm calling. Would you be terribly upset if we canceled tonight?"

"Of course not," she says, sitting up. "Is everything okay?"

"Everything's fine. Mom's just kind of dragging after her doctor's appointment this afternoon. To tell you the truth, so am I."

"Do you want me to pick up something from Pazzano's and drop it off? I'd be happy to."

"That's sweet of you, but no, we're good. I'm going to reheat some lasagna and we're hitting the sack early."

"Okay, but call me if you change your mind. And give Mom my best."

"I will, honey. Thanks for being such a great daughter."

"'Night, Dad."

Gwendy hangs up and looks at the Christmas tree standing in the corner. A string of lights has gone out. "Yeah, some great daughter . . . I completely forgot she even had a doctor's appointment today." She gets up and takes a couple of steps into the middle of the room, and then stops. Suddenly, she wants to cry, and not just your garden variety sniffles, either. She feels like dropping to her knees, burying her face in her hands, and sobbing until she passes out.

A tightness growing in her chest, Gwendy slumps onto the sofa again. *This is pathetic*, she thinks, wiping away tears with the heels of her hands. *Absolutely pathetic. Maybe a hot bath and a glass of wine will*—

And then she looks at the button box.

37

GWENDY CAN'T REMEMBER THE last time she went on two runs in the same day. If she had to guess, she'd say it was the summer when she was twelve years old, the same summer Frankie Stone started calling her Goodyear and she finally decided to do something about her weight. She ran pretty much everywhere that summer—to the corner store to pick up eggs and bread for her mother, to Olive's house to listen to records and tear through the latest issue of *Teen* magazine, and of course, every morning (even on Sundays) she ran the Suicide Stairs up to Castle View Park. By the time school started in September, Gwendy had lost almost fifteen pounds of baby fat and the button box was hidden away in the bottom of her bedroom closet. After that, life would never be the same for her.

Tonight, she jogs at a fast clip along the centerline of Route 117, enjoying the feel of her heart pounding in her chest. The snow stopped falling several hours earlier, right around dinnertime, and the plows are busy clearing side streets at this late hour. The main roadways are eerily empty and hushed. At the bottom of the hill, she passes a group of men wearing hardhats and orange vests with CRPW stenciled on them: *Castle Rock Public Works*. One of them drops the shovel he's working and gives her an enthusiastic round of applause. She flashes the man a smile and a thumbs-up, and keeps on trucking.

The tiny piece of chocolate the button box dispensed was

in the shape of an owl, and Gwendy stared in rapt fascination at the amazing details—the staggered lines of each feather, the pointy tip of its beak, the pools of dark shadow that made up its eyes—before popping it into her mouth and allowing it to dissolve on her tongue.

There was a moment of complete *satisfaction*—at what, she didn't know, maybe *everything*—and then a rush of startling clarity and energy spread throughout her body. All of a sudden, she not only no longer felt like crying, her entire body felt lighter, her vision seemed clearer, and the colors in the condo appeared brighter and more vibrant. Was this what it was like when she was younger? She couldn't exactly remember. All she knew was that it suddenly felt like she'd sprouted wings and could fly up into the sky and touch the moon. She immediately changed into workout clothes and running shoes, and headed outside.

No, not immediately, she reminds herself, as she cruises past the Sunoco station toward Main Street and the center of town.

Something else happened first.

In the midst of all those good feelings, those *wonderful* feelings, she suddenly found herself fixating on the red button at the left side of the box, and then slowly reaching out with a finger and touching it, caressing its glassy surface, and the thought of actually pressing it and erasing President Richard Hamlin from the face of the earth wormed inside the basement of her brain like the wisp of a forgotten dream just before waking.

Whoa, girl, a little voice whispered inside her head. *Be careful what you daydream because that box can hear you thinking. Don't you doubt it, not even for a second.*

Then, and only then, did she carefully withdraw her finger and go upstairs to change into running gear.

38

THE NEXT DAY DAWNS clear and cold. A brisk wind blows in from the east, swirling amongst the treetops and drifting mounds of snow against the tires of parked cars and the sides of buildings. In the glare of morning sun, the blanket of ice-crusted snow is almost too brilliant to look at.

Gwendy pulls her car to the shoulder of the narrow back road and takes off her sunglasses. A half-dozen sheriff's department vehicles are parked in a staggered line in front of her. A group of uniformed officers huddle between two of the cars, heads down, lost in conversation. An open field of maybe fifteen or twenty acres bordered by deep woods stretches out along the right side of the road. Thick trees crowd the other side, blocking the sun's rays and dropping the temperature there by at least ten degrees.

Sheriff Ridgewick spots her car and disengages from the other men. He starts walking in her direction, so Gwendy gets out and meets him halfway.

"Thanks for coming on short notice," he says. "I thought you'd want to be here."

"What's going on?" she asks, zipping up her heavy jacket. "Did you find the girls?"

"No." He looks out across the open field. "Not yet. But we did find the sweatshirt Carla Hoffman was wearing the night she disappeared."

She looks around. "All the way out here?"

He nods and points at the northeast corner of the field. Gwendy follows his finger and, squinting, she can just make out a couple of dark figures camouflaged by the backdrop of trees. "One of my men spotted it this morning. Wind was blowing so hard it was actually moving across the field. That's what caught his attention. That and the color."

"Color?"

"We knew from talking to Carla's older brother that she'd been wearing a pink Nike sweatshirt the night she was taken. The officer saw something small and pink tumbling across the field and pulled over. At first he thought it was just a plastic grocery bag. Wind blows hard like today, these trees act like a kind of wind tunnel and all kind of crap flies through here. Empty cans. Fast food litter. Plastic bags, paper bags, you name it."

"Sounds like your officer deserves a raise for checking it out."

"He's a good man." The sheriff looks closely at Gwendy. "All of my men and women are."

"So what happens next?"

"Evidence is out there now looking at the sweatshirt. Deputy Footman's pulling in some additional bodies to conduct a search of the surrounding area. You're welcome to help if you'd like. Half the town will probably show up if we let 'em."

Gwendy nods her head. "I think I will. I have a hat and gloves in the car."

"Helluva way to spend the day before Christmas Eve." He sighs deeply. "Anyway, probably another hour or so before we get started. Might as well get inside and run the heater." He starts back toward the other men. "There's coffee and donuts in one of the patrol cars if you want."

Gwendy doesn't acknowledge the offer. She's staring at the snow-covered field, her brow furrowed. "Sheriff . . . if your deputy found the sweatshirt blowing around on top of the snow, and it just stopped snowing yesterday afternoon sometime, that means the sweatshirt was left sometime in the last . . ." She thinks. "Sixteen hours, give or take."

"Maybe," he says. "Unless it was somewhere under cover and the wind shook it loose after the snow stopped."

"Huh," Gwendy says. "I didn't think of that."

"All I know is there are no houses within three miles of us and this stretch of road is mainly used by hunters. The sweatshirt either found us by accident or we were meant to find it." He glances at the men huddled between the cars and then looks back at Gwendy. "My money's on the second one."

39

SHERIFF RIDGEWICK IS RIGHT about one thing: half the town of Castle Rock shows up for the search. At least, that's how it appears to Gwendy as she takes her place in the long, arcing line of locals, most of the women dressed in colorful winter coats and boots, most of the men wearing the standard autumn uniform of an adult New England male—camouflage. As they begin fanning out across the field, Gwendy looks around and sees old folks walking alongside young couples, and young couples walking alongside college and high school kids. Even under these dreary circumstances, the sight brings a brief smile to her face. For all of its dark history and idiosyncrasies, Castle Rock is still a place that takes care of its own.

The sheriff's instructions to the group are simple enough: walk slowly, side by side, with no more than five or six feet separating you from the person on your right and the person on your left; if you find something, anything, don't touch it and don't get too close, call for one of the officers and they'll come running.

Gwendy stares at the snow-covered terrain in front of her, willing her feet to move deliberately, despite the frigid temperature pushing her to pick up the pace. Her cheeks burn and her eyes water from the constant gusts of wind. For the first time that morning, her thoughts stray to the button box. She knows that eating the chocolate was a mistake, a moment of weakness,

RICHARD CHIZMAR

and is determined not to allow it to happen again. Sure, it made her feel better last night—okay, it did much more than that, if she's being perfectly honest with herself. And when she looked in the bathroom mirror this morning—feeling more rested and purer in soul than she's felt in months—and noticed the dark circles that had taken up residence under her eyes the past few weeks had vanished, all of a sudden the magic chocolates didn't seem like such a bad idea after all.

But then she remembered her finger brushing against the smooth surface of the red button and that little voice whispering inside her head—*Be careful what you daydream because that box can hear you thinking*—and she shuddered at the memory and tried her best to push it far, far away.

"Gwendy, dear," a voice says, startling her from her thoughts. "How is your mother doing?"

Gwendy cranes her head forward and looks first to her right, and then to her left. An older woman, a few spots down the line, lifts a gloved hand and waves.

"Mrs. Verrill! I didn't even see you there."

The woman smiles back at her. "That's okay, dear. It's hard to tell who's who all bundled up like this."

"Mom's doing much better. Thank you for asking. She's back in the kitchen and ready to kick my father out of the house so she can have some peace and quiet."

Mrs. Verrill lifts a hand to her mouth and chuckles. "Well, please tell her I said hello and that I would love to stop by and see her sometime."

"I'll do that, Mrs. Verrill. I'm sure she'd be thrilled to see you."

"Thank you, dear."

Gwendy smiles and returns her focus to the field of untouched snow stretching out before her. She guesses it's maybe another fifty or sixty yards before they reach the tree line. *Then what?* she thinks. *Do we turn around or plow ahead?* She must have missed that part of Sheriff Ridgewick's—

Sensing that the man walking to her immediate right is staring at her, Gwendy glances in his direction. She's right; his brown eyes are closely studying her. The man is young, early twenties, and underdressed in an untucked flannel shirt and Buffalo Bills baseball cap. He suddenly grins and looks right past her. "I told you it was her, Pops."

"Excuse me?" she says, confused.

A quiet voice from her left says, "I thought for sure she was too young to be a governor . . . or senator."

Gwendy looks from her left to her right and back again. "I'm . . . I'm not either one."

The older man scratches at his unshaven chin. "Then what are ya?"

"I'm a—"

"She's a congresswoman," the young man says with a look of embarrassment. "I told you that."

"I'm afraid you two have lost me," Gwendy says, exasperated. "Have we met before?"

"No, ma'am. My name is Lucas Browne and that there's my father."

"Charlie," the other man says, placing his hand on his stomach and giving a little bow. "Third generation Castle Rock."

"Wait a minute, so your name is . . . Charlie Browne?"

He bows again. "At your service."

The younger man groans and blushes an even deeper shade of red.

They're actually kind of charming, Gwendy thinks.

"Anyway, I saw you standing there when the sheriff was

talking," Lucas says. "I nudged my Pops and told him who you were." He looks at his father with a raised chin. "But he didn't believe me."

"I didn't, I admit it," he says, hands raised. "I thought you had to be a lot older to work high up in the government like that."

Gwendy gives him a big smile. "Well, I'll take that as a compliment. Thank you."

Beaming, the older man puffs his chest out. "My boy there, he's the smart one in the family. Two years of college down in Buffalo . . . before he ran into a bit of trouble. But he'll go back and finish what he started one day soon. Ain't that right, son?"

Lucas, suddenly looking like he'd rather be anywhere else in the world right then, nods his head. "Yes, sir. One day."

"Well, it's a pleasure to meet you both," Gwendy says, anxious to move on from the conversation. "It's always nice to get to know—"

"What's that?" Lucas asks, pointing at a small dark object emerging from the trees in front of them. A murmur of raised voices travels down the line of searchers. People start pointing. Someone on the far left flank breaks formation and chases after the object, slipping and sprawling face-first in the snow. Several people sarcastically cheer.

At first, Gwendy thinks it's a plastic grocery bag, like the sheriff had described earlier. It's the right size and shape, and it's riding the wind's currents, up, down, swirling in tight little circles, tumbling wildly to the ground, and then surfing back up again.

But then, halfway across the open field, the object appears to inexplicably change direction in mid-flight. Banking hard to the right, it heads directly toward her

—and Gwendy flashes back to a blustery golden-hued April afternoon she once spent at the side of a boy she loved, flying kites and holding hands and feeling like their happiness would last forever and—

at that moment, she understands it's a hat swooping toward her in the whipping wind—a small, neat black hat.

The dark object suddenly veers to the left, hurtling away from her at terrific speed, and for one fleeting, hopeful moment, Gwendy believes she's wrong, it's just a grocery bag after all—but then the wind squalls again and it loops back around, coming closer and closer, swerving and somersaulting across the frozen ground directly at her feet—

—where Lucas Browne leaps forward and stomps on it, abruptly halting its long journey.

"Would you look at that?" Charlie Browne says, eyes wide as 1891 silver dollars. He bends down to pick it up.

"Stop!" Gwendy shouts. "Don't touch it!"

The older man jerks his hand back and looks up at her. "Why not?"

"It . . . it could be evidence."

"Oh, yeah," he says, straightening up and smacking himself a good one on the side of his head.

A small crowd has gathered around them by now.

"What is it?"

"Is that what I think it is?"

"Did you see that sucker move? Almost like someone was working a remote control."

Deputy Footman sidesteps his way through the group of onlookers. "What've you got there?"

"Sorry about that, officer," Lucas says, removing his boot from the object. "Only way I could stop it."

The deputy doesn't say anything. He drops to a knee in the snow and carefully examines the object.

It's not a grocery bag, of course.

It's a hat—a small, neat black hat.

Faded with age, tattered and worn around the edges of the brim, a ragged three-inch tear slicing across the top of the crushed dome.

"This thing's been out here forever," the deputy says, rising to his feet. "It's no help to us." He walks away, and the crowd begins to dissipate.

Gwendy doesn't move. Biting her lip, she stares down at the black hat, almost hypnotized by the sight of it, unaware that Charlie Browne and his son are watching her. *Is Farris sending some kind of a message? Or is he playing games with me? Making up for lost time?*

She bends down to get a better look at the filthy hat— and a gust of wind picks it up and swoops it away from her, sending it hurtling toward the road. It climbs and climbs, then plummets to the ground, rolling on its side like a child's Frisbee for several yards before lifting up and taking flight once again.

Gwendy stands in the middle of the snow-covered field, eyes lifted to the sky, and watches as the black hat disappears into the trees beyond the road. When she turns around, the staggered human chain of searchers has moved on without her.

40

HOMELAND CEMETERY IS THE largest and prettiest of Castle Rock's three graveyards. There are tall iron gates out front with a lock, but it's used only twice a year—on graduation night at the high school and on Halloween. Sheriff George Bannerman is buried in Homeland, as is Reginald "Pop" Merrill, one of the town's most infamous—and unsavory—citizens.

Gwendy drives through the ornate gates just as dusk is settling over the land, and she can't decide whether the cemetery, with its rolling hills and stone monuments and lengthening shadows, appears tranquil or menacing. Maybe both, she decides, parking along the central lane and getting out. Maybe both.

Knowing where she's going, she walks a direct route, punching her way through knee-deep snow to a scattering of grave markers that rest atop a steep hillside skirted by a small grove of pine trees. There are smudges of naked earth here where the tree's thick branches have prevented snow from accumulating below. The treetops sway back and forth overhead, whispering secrets to each other in the cold breeze.

Gwendy stops in front of a small marker in the last row. The trees grow close together, blocking the day's dying light and casting the ground in shadow, but she knows what's carved onto the headstone by memory:

OLIVE GRACE KEPNES
1962-1979
Our Loving Angel

She drops to a knee in the snow, only several inches deep here, and traces the grooves with her bare fingertips. As always, she thinks whoever was in charge of the inscription did a pretty shitty job of it. Where were the exact dates of Olive's birth and death? Those were important days to remember and should have been included. And what did "Our Loving Angel" have to say about the *real* Olive Kepnes? Nothing. It said nothing at all to keep her memory alive. Why didn't it mention that Olive had an infectious laugh and knew more about Peter Frampton than anyone else in the world? Or that she was a connoisseur of all types of candy and bad horror movies on late night television? Or that she wanted to be a veterinarian when she grew up?

Gwendy kneels in the snow—feet numb despite her waterproof boots thanks to hours of fruitless searching earlier in the afternoon—and visits with her old friend until the pools of shadow melt together into one, and then she says goodbye and slowly walks back in the dark to her car.

41

GWENDY LOCKS THE CAR and is halfway up the sidewalk to her condo when she hears footsteps behind her.

She glances over her shoulder, scanning the length of parking lot. At first she doesn't see anyone, even though she can still hear the hurried footfalls. Then she spots him: a man, lost in the shadows between streetlights, striding toward her. Maybe thirty yards away and moving fast.

Gwendy hurries to the entrance and punches in her security code with shaky fingers. She tries to open the door but it doesn't budge.

She looks behind her again, panicking now. The man is closer. Maybe fifteen yards away. She can't be a hundred percent certain in the dark, but it looks like he's wearing a ski mask, obscuring his face. Just like in her dream.

Gwendy punches in the code again, concentrating on each button. The door buzzes. She flings it open, steps inside, and slams it shut behind her, sprinting up the stairs to the second floor. As she fumbles with her keys outside the door to her condo, she hears someone rattling the entrance door downstairs, trying to get in.

She finally gets the door unlocked and rushes inside. After locking the deadbolt, she hurries to the front window and takes a peek outside.

The parking lot is empty. The man is nowhere in sight.

42

"Morning, Sheila," Gwendy says, a little too eager for the early hour. "I'm here to see Sheriff Ridgewick."

The scarecrow-thin woman with bright red hair and matching eyeglasses looks up from the magazine she's reading. "Hey there, Gwendy. Sorry I missed you the other day. Heard there was some fireworks."

Sheila Brigham has manned the glass-walled dispatch cubicle at the Castle County Sheriff's Department for going on twenty-five years now. She's also in charge of the front desk and coffee maker. Sheila started on the job fresh out of community college, when bell-bottoms were all the rage and George Bannerman was patrolling The Rock. She got married and raised a family here, and took good care of Alan Pangborn during his decade-long stint, and, unlike most folks, didn't let the fire of '91 scare her away, even though she'd spent nearly three weeks in a hospital bed in the aftermath of that disaster.

"I'm afraid I didn't inspire much confidence in our elected officials," Gwendy says.

Sheila waves a dismissive hand. "Don't worry yourself none about that. Carol Hoffman's mean as a hornet on a good day—and she doesn't have many of those."

"Still, I feel horrible. That poor woman."

Sheila makes a grunting sound. "You want to feel sorry for someone, feel sorry for that husband of hers."

"Can't argue with you there."

She picks up her magazine again. "You can go on back. He's waiting for you."

"Thank you. Merry Christmas, Sheila."

She makes that same grunting sound and returns her attention to reading.

The door to Sheriff Ridgewick's office is open, so Gwendy walks right in. He's sitting behind his desk talking on the telephone. He holds up a finger, mouths "one minute," and gestures for her to sit down. "I understand that, Jay, I do. But we don't have time. I need it yesterday." His face darkens. "I don't care. Just get it done."

He hangs up and looks at Gwendy. "Sorry about that."

"No problem," she says. "Now what's all the secrecy about? Why couldn't you just tell me on the phone?"

The sheriff shakes his head. "Don't like that cellphone of yours. Last thing we need right now is a leak."

"You're as paranoid as my father. He's whipped himself into a frenzy. Thinks all the world's technology's going to collapse when the clock strikes midnight next week."

"Tell that to Tommy Perkins. He claims he picks up a half-dozen cellphone conversations every day on that short-wave of his."

Gwendy laughs. "Tom Perkins is a dirty-minded, senile old man. You really believe what he says?"

The sheriff shrugs. "How else did he know about Shelly Piper being pregnant before the rest of the town?"

"Probably did the deed himself, the old perv."

The sheriff's jaw drops, his mouth forming a perfect O. "Gwendy Peterson."

"Oh, hush," she says, waving a hand at him. "And stop stalling, Norris. Is the news that bad?"

The smile fades from his face. "I'm afraid it is."

"Tell me."

He gets up and closes the door. Returning to his desk, he opens a drawer and takes out a large envelope. "Take a look," he says, handing it to Gwendy.

She opens the flap and slides out a pair of glossy color photographs. It's hard to tell what the three small white objects are in the first photo, but the second shot is a close-up view and much clearer. "Teeth?" she says, looking at the sheriff.

He nods in response.

"Where'd they come from?"

"They were found inside the pocket of Carla Hoffman's pink sweatshirt."

43

GWENDY'S STILL THINKING ABOUT the three small teeth hours later as she showers and gets ready to attend Christmas Eve mass with her parents.

Forensics have already confirmed that the teeth are archetypal for a female Carla Hoffman's age, and Sheriff Ridgewick's in touch with the girl's dental office to determine if they have X-rays on file. Carla's parents know about the sweatshirt but haven't been told about the gruesome discovery made inside the pocket. "It's our first concrete piece of evidence," the sheriff had confided to Gwendy. "We need to see where it leads before news of it gets blabbed all over town."

The discovery of the teeth had pushed thoughts of last night's terrifying encounter in the parking lot out of Gwendy's mind, but they return to her now, twenty-four hours later, as she's selecting a dress for church.

The whole thing feels like a bad dream. The man was wearing a mask, she's sure of that now. But at this time of year, ski masks are common. Other than that, she doesn't remember much of anything. Dark clothing, maybe jeans, and some kind of shoes or boots with a heel. She definitely heard him before she saw him. Another thing, she hadn't noticed any strange cars in the lot, so he either parked somewhere nearby and came in on foot, or he lived close by.

But why would anyone want to do that? she thinks, settling on a long black dress and a pair of leather boots. *Was he just trying to scare her? Or was it more than that? For that matter, did he even know it was* her? *Maybe the whole thing was just a prank. Or had nothing to do with her at all.*

Gwendy also wonders why she chose not to say anything about it to Sheriff Ridgewick this morning, although she has a theory about that. It all points back to the chocolate owl she ate a couple of nights earlier. It's true that eating the chocolate immediately infused her with a sense of calm energy and clearness of vision—both the internal and external variety—but it did more than that: it gave her back her sense of balance in the world; a sense of confidence that was sorely lacking these past few months. Missing Ryan, floundering at her job, worrying about her mom and a President with the IQ of a turnip and the temperament of a schoolyard bully . . . all of a sudden, she felt like she could shoulder her share of the load again, and more. *All thanks to some kind of wonder drug . . . or candy,* she thinks. It was an uneasy feeling to have, and in some ways it made her feel even guiltier about eating the chocolate. After all, she wasn't a lost and insecure teenager like the first time the button box came into her life. She was an adult now with years of experience at handling the curve balls life threw at her.

She's strapping on her seat belt and pulling out of the parking lot on her way to meet her parents at church when that dreaded question rears its ugly head once again: *How much of her life is her own doing, and how much the doing of the box with its treats and buttons?*

Gwendy has never been less sure of the answer.

44

FOR AS LONG AS Gwendy can remember, the Petersons have attended the 7:00 PM Christmas Eve mass at Our Lady of Serene Waters Catholic Church, and then gone crosstown to the Bradleys' annual holiday party afterward. When she was a little girl, Gwendy would often spend the drowsy drive home with her head resting against the cool glass of her back-seat window, searching the night sky for a glimpse of Rudolph's glowing red nose.

The church service tonight lasts a little more than an hour. Hugh and Blanche Goff, the Petersons' longtime next-door neighbors, arrive a few minutes late. Gwendy happily scoots over to make room for them in the pew. Mrs. Goff smells like mothballs and peppermint breath mints, but Gwendy doesn't mind. The Goffs were never able to have children of their own, and she's like a surrogate daughter to them.

Gwendy closes her eyes and loses herself in Father Lawrence's sermon, his soothing voice as much a part of her childhood memories as Saturday morning swims with Olive Kepnes at the Castle Rock Rec Pool. Few of the priest's stories are new to her, but she finds his words and delivery comforting nonetheless. Gwendy watches the simple joy in her mother's face as Mrs. Peterson sings along with the choir and, a short time later, stifles a giggle when Mr. Goff breaks wind during Holy Communion, earning a gentle elbow to the ribs from her father.

When the service is over, the Petersons file out with the rest of the congregation and stand outside of the church's main entrance, mingling with friends and neighbors. The most boisterous greetings are reserved for Gwendy's mom, as this is her first time back at church in weeks. There is one exception, however. Father Lawrence wraps Gwendy up in a bear hug and actually lifts her off the ground. Before he disappears back into the rectory, he makes her promise to come back soon. Once the crowd thins out, Gwendy walks Mr. and Mrs. Goff to their car in the parking lot, and then she follows her parents to the Bradleys' mansion on Willow Street.

Anita Bradley—as Castle Rock gossips have enviously whispered for going on three decades now—married old and married rich. After her husband Lester, a wildly successful lumber tycoon nineteen years her senior, suffered a fatal heart attack in early 1991, many locals thought that once the funeral services were completed and legal matters attended to, Anita would pack up house and head for the sunny shores of Florida or maybe even an island somewhere. But they were wrong. Castle Rock was her home, Anita insisted, and she wasn't going anywhere.

As it turns out, her staying was a very good thing for the town. Anita has spent the almost nine years since her husband's death donating her time and money to a long list of local charities, volunteering her sewing expertise to help out the Castle Rock High School Theatrical Society, and serving as the head of the library's Board of Trustees. She also makes a ridiculously delicious apple pie, which she sells at Nora's Bake Shop all summer long.

A smiling and moderately tipsy Anita—her long, thick gray hair styled into some kind of gravity-defeating, triple-decker, power tower—welcomes the Peterson family inside her home with dainty hugs and papery soft (not to mention, sandpapery dry) kisses on their cheeks. The three-story Bradley house sprawls more than seven thousand square feet atop the rocky hillside and is filled with room after room of turn-of-the-century antiques. Gwendy has always been terrified of breaking something valuable. She takes her parents' coats and, adding her own, leaves them draped over a Victorian sofa in the library. Then she heads into the bustling, high-ceiled great room, searching for familiar faces, anxious to make an appearance and get back home again.

But, as is often the case in Castle Rock, familiar faces her age prove difficult to find. Most of Gwendy's close friends from high school never returned to The Rock after attending college. Like her, many of them took jobs in nearby Portland or Derry or Bangor. Others moved to distant states, only returning for occasional visits with parents or siblings. Brigette Desjardin is one of only a small handful of exceptions to this rule, and appears to be the only one in attendance here at the Bradleys' annual Christmas party. Gwendy bumps into her by the punch bowl—there are no unfortunate spills this time around—and enjoys a spirited but brief conversation with Brigette and her husband Travis before a PTA friend of Brigette's drunkenly interrupts them. Gwendy smiles and moves on.

Of course, there are plenty of others waiting to speak with Gwendy. While familiar faces are scarce, friendly—and merely curious—faces are not. It seems as if everyone there wants a photo or a quick word or two with the Celebrity Congresswoman, and the barrage of questions comes fast and furious:

Where's your husband? Where's Ryan? ("Overseas working on assignment.")

How's your mom feeling? ("Much better, thank you, she's here somewhere, I'm actually trying to find her.")

What's President Hamlin really like? ("Ummm . . . he's a handful.")

How's it going down there in DC? ("Oh, it's going okay, trying to fight the good fight every day.")

Why aren't you drinking? Hold on, let me grab you something. ("No, thanks, really, I'm kind of tired and not much of a drinker.")

What about those missing girls? ("It's terrible and it's frightening, and I know the sheriff and his people are doing everything humanly possible to find them.")

I saw you running the other night. Don't you ever get tired of all that running? ("Actually, no, I find it relaxing—that's why I do it.")

How worried should I be about what's going on with North Korea? Do you think we're going to war? ("Don't lose any sleep over it. A lot of awfully bad things would have to happen for the United States to go to war, and I don't believe it's going to happen.") Gwendy's not so sure about this last one, but she figures it's part of her job to keep her constituents calm.

By the time she locates her parents sitting in a corner on the opposite side of the room talking to a co-worker from Dad's office (the man also requests a "real quick photo," which Gwendy dutifully smiles for), she feels like she's just finished an all-day publicity whirlwind for one of her book releases. She also has a splitting headache.

Once they're alone, she tells her parents she's exhausted and asks if they'll be okay at the party without her. Her mom fusses that Gwendy needs to stop working so hard and orders her right home to bed. Her father gives her a sarcastic look and says, "I think we can survive without your guiding light for one night, kiddo. Go home and get some rest." Gwendy swats him on the arm, kisses them both goodnight, and starts across the room toward the library to get her coat.

That's when it happens.

A muscular hand reaches out from the sea of people and grabs Gwendy by the shoulder, spinning her around.

"Well, well, well, look who it is."

Caroline Hoffman suddenly looms in front of her, bloodshot eyes narrowed into slits. The hand gripping Gwendy's shoulder begins to squeeze. Her free hand balls into a meaty fist.

Gwendy glances around the room, looking for help . . . but Mr. Hoffman is nowhere in sight, and none of the other partygoers seem to have noticed what's happening. "Mrs. Hoffman, I don't know what—"

"You make me sick, you know that?"

"Well, I'm sorry you feel that way, but I don't know—"

The hand squeezes harder.

"Let go of me," Gwendy says, shrugging the woman's hand off of her. She can smell Mrs. Hoffman's breath—and not beer, the hard stuff. The last thing she wants to do is antagonize her. "Listen, I appreciate the fact that you're upset and you don't like me very much, but this isn't the time or the place."

"I think it's the perfect time and place," Mrs. Hoffman says, an ugly sneer spreading across her face.

"For what?" Gwendy asks heavily.

"For me to kick your stuck-up little ass."

Gwendy takes a step back, raising her hands in front of her, in shock that this is actually happening.

"Is everything okay?" a tall man Gwendy has never seen before asks.

"No," she says, voice trembling. "No, it's not. This woman has had too much to drink and needs a ride home. Can you help her find someone? Or perhaps you can call her husband?"

"I'd be happy to." The man turns to Mrs. Hoffman and tries to take her arm. She shoves him away. He slams into a couple behind him, knocking the other man's wineglass out of his hand. It tumbles to the floor and shatters—and now everyone in the room is staring at the tall stranger and Mrs. Hoffman.

"What are y'all gawking at?!" she slurs, the color rising in her chubby cheeks. "Buncha blue-ballers!"

"Oh, my," someone behind Gwendy says.

Gwendy takes advantage of the distraction and quickly slips away into the library where she digs out her coat from the now massive pile on the sofa. She puts it on, rubbing away furious tears, and starts pacing in front of the sofa. *How dare she put her hands on me? How dare she say those things?* Pacing faster now, she can feel the heat intensifying throughout her body. *All I was trying to do was help her rude ass and she acts like—*

A loud crash comes from the next room.

And then cries of alarm.

Gwendy hurries back into the great room, afraid of what she might find.

Caroline Hoffman is lying unconscious on the hardwood floor, her arms splayed above her head. A nasty gash on her forehead is bleeding heavily. A crowd has gathered around her.

"What happened?" Gwendy asks no one in particular.

"She fell," an old man, standing in front of her, says. "She'd calmed down some and was walking out on her own and she just spun around and fell and hit her head on the table. Darnedest thing I've ever seen."

"It was almost like somebody pushed her," another woman says. "But there wasn't anybody there."

Remembering the flush of anger she'd just experienced and a long-forgotten dream about Frankie Stone, Gwendy stumbles out of the house in a daze and doesn't look back.

Head spinning, it takes her several minutes to remember where she parked her car. When she finally locates it near the bottom of the Bradleys' long driveway, she gets in and drives home in silence.

45

WHEN GWENDY GETS HOME fifteen minutes later, she changes into a nightgown, washes her face and brushes her teeth, and goes directly to bed. She doesn't turn on the television, she doesn't put her cellphone on charge, and for the first time since its return, she leaves the button box locked inside the safe overnight.

46

GWENDY DOESN'T CHECK ON the button box the next morning, either. Another first for her.

Christmas dawns dark and gloomy with a suffocating layer of thick clouds hanging over Castle Rock. The weather forecast calls for snow by nightfall, and the town DPW trucks are already busy dropping salt as Gwendy makes her way down Route 117 to her parents' house. Almost all of the homes she passes still have their Christmas lights glowing at ten-thirty in the morning. For some reason, instead of looking cheerful and festive, the dim lights and murky sky provide a depressing backdrop to her drive.

Gwendy expects to pass the day in the same blue mood she went to bed with but is determined to hide it from her parents. They have enough on their plate without her ruining their Christmas celebration.

But by the time the brunch table is cleared and presents are exchanged in the living room, Gwendy finds herself in a surprisingly cheery mood. Something about spending Christmas morning in the house she grew up in makes the world feel safe and small again, if only for a short time.

As they do every year, Mr. and Mrs. Peterson fret about Gwendy going overboard and spoiling them with gifts—"We asked you not to do that this year, honey, we didn't have much time to get out and shop!"—but she can tell they're surprised and pleased with her choices. Dad, still dressed in a robe and pajamas, sits in his recliner with his legs up, reading the instructions for his brand-new DVD player. Mom is busy modeling her L.L.Bean jacket and boots in the full-length hallway mirror. A stack of jigsaw puzzles, assorted shirts and sweaters, a TiVo so Mom can digitally record her shows, a men's L.L.Bean winter jacket, and subscription gift cards to *National Geographic* and *People* magazine sit under the tree, next to Ryan's unopened presents.

Gwendy is equally pleased with her own gifts, particularly a gorgeous leather-bound journal her mother found in a small shop in Bangor. She's sitting on the living-room sofa, relishing the texture of the thick paper against her fingertips, when her father reaches out with a large red envelope in his hand.

"One more little present, Gwennie."

"What's this?" she asks, taking the envelope.

"A surprise," Mrs. Peterson says, coming over and sitting on the arm of her husband's recliner.

Gwendy opens the envelope and slides out a card. A glittery Christmas tree decorates the front of it. A little girl with pigtails stands at the foot of the tree, looking up with wonder in her eyes. Gwendy opens the card—and a small white feather spills out and flutters to the carpet at her feet.

"Is that—?" she starts to ask, eyes wide, and then she reads what her father has written inside the card . . .

> You have ALWAYS
> believed in magic,
> dear Gwendy, and magic
> has ALWAYS believed
> in you.

. . . and she can no longer find the words to finish.

She looks up at her parents. They're both sitting there with goofy grins on their faces. Happy tears are forming in her mother's eyes.

Gwendy bends down and picks up the feather, stares at it with disbelief. "I just can't . . ." She turns the feather over in her hand. "How did you . . . *where* did you find it?"

"I found it in the garage," her father says proudly. "I was looking for a 3/8 inch screw in one of those cabinets you liked to play with so much when you were little, the ones with all the little drawers?"

Gwendy mutely nods her head.

"Slid out the last drawer in the last row, and there it was. I couldn't believe it myself."

"You must have hidden it there," her mother says. "What? Almost thirty years ago."

"I don't remember," Gwendy says. She looks up at her parents and this time she's the one wearing the big goofy grin. "I can't believe you found my magic feather . . ."

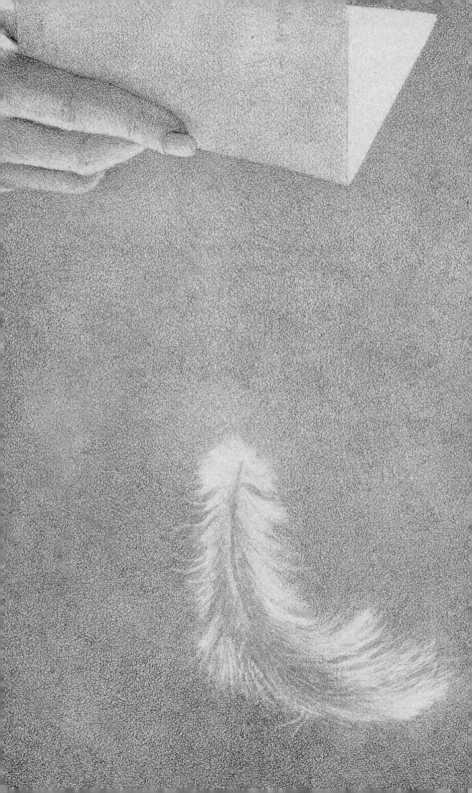

47

WHEN GWENDY IS TEN *years old, her family spends a week in upstate New York visiting with one of Mr. Peterson's first cousins. It's July and the cousin (Gwendy can no longer remember his name nor the names of his wife or three children; as best as she can recall, they never saw them again except at the occasional wedding or funeral) has a summer home on a lake, so there's plenty to do. Canoeing, swimming, fishing, jumping off tire swings, even water skiing. There's also a small town nearby with a mini golf course and water slide for the tourists.*

Gwendy looks forward to the trip all summer long. She starts saving her money as soon as the school year ends, stashing away the quarters she makes from helping her father clean the garage and dusting the house from top to bottom for her mother. By the time she packs her own suitcase and climbs into the back seat for the seven-hour drive, she's managed to save almost fifteen dollars in loose change. Her plan is to hold onto most of the money until the final two days of the trip, and then splurge on herself. Candy, comics, ice cream, maybe even a pocket transistor radio with an earphone if she has enough left over.

But it doesn't work out that way.

Within minutes of their arrival, Mr. and Mrs. Peterson disappear into the cabin for a "grand tour" and Gwendy finds herself standing by the car surrounded by a group of local kids, including the cousin's three children, who are all spending the summer at the lake. The boys are shirtless and tan and look wild with their messy hair and sugar-spiked eyes. The girls are long-legged and aloof and mostly older.

Nervous and not knowing what else to say, Gwendy eventually unzips her suitcase and shows the kids her plastic marble bag filled with quarters. Most of them are indifferent, and a few even laugh at her. But one of the older boys doesn't laugh; he seems interested, and maybe even impressed. He waits until the other kids all run off, whooping and hollering into the back yard, and then he approaches Gwendy.

"Hey, kid," he says, looking around. "I got something you might be interested in."

"What?" Gwendy asks, even more nervous now that she's alone with a boy—a cute, older boy.

He reaches into the back pocket of his cut-off jean shorts and when his hand swims back into view, it's holding something small and fluffy and white.

"A feather?" Gwendy asks, confused.

A look of disgust comes onto the older boy's face. "Not just any old feather. It's a magic feather."

Gwendy feels her heart flutter. "Magic?"

"That's right. It once belonged to an Indian chief who used to live around here. He was also a medicine man, a very powerful one."

Gwendy swallows. "What does it do?"

"It does . . . magic stuff," he says. "You know, like bringing you good luck and making you smarter. Stuff like that."

"Can I hold it?" Gwendy asks almost breathlessly.

"Sure, but I'm getting kinda tired of taking care of it. I've had it for a few years now. You interested in taking it off my hands?"

"You want to give it to me?"

"Not give," he says. "Sell."

Gwendy doesn't miss a beat. "How much?"

The boy lifts a dirty finger to his lips, thinking. "I guess ten dollars is a fair enough price."

Gwendy's shoulders sag a little. "I don't know . . . that's a lot of money."

RICHARD CHIZMAR

"Not for a magic feather it ain't." He starts to put the feather back in his pocket. "No biggie, I'll just sell it to someone else."

"Wait," Gwendy blurts. "I didn't say no."

He looks down his nose at her. "You didn't say yes either."

Gwendy glances at the plastic bag filled with quarters and then looks at the feather again.

"Tell you what," the boy says. "You're new around here, so I'll cut you a deal. How's nine dollars sound?"

Gwendy feels as if she's just won the grand prize at the spinning wheel booth at the Castle Rock Fourth of July carnival. "Deal," she says at once, and starts counting out nine dollars in quarters.

48

DRIVING HOME LATER THAT Christmas night, Gwendy thinks about her father's words from earlier: "We all poked fun at you about that feather, Gwen, but you didn't care. You *believed*. That's what mattered then, and that's what matters now: you've always been a believer. That beautiful heart of yours has led you down some unexpected roads, but your faith—in yourself, in others, in the world around you—has always guided you. That's what that magic feather of yours stands for."

49

UNFORTUNATELY, EVEN AFTER THE surprise appearance of her long-lost magic feather, Gwendy's good mood doesn't last, and by nine o'clock, she's slumped in front of the television, missing her husband terribly. A hollow ache has crept into her heart, and no amount of meditation or happy-sappy positive thinking can ease it. She stares at her cellphone, willing it to ring, but it remains silent on the sofa beside her.

The button box sits on the coffee table next to her Grisham book, the small white feather, and a cup of hot tea. Normally, Gwendy would be worried about spilling her drink and getting it on the box. Tonight she doesn't give a damn.

Once she got back to the condo, Gwendy called Sheriff Ridgewick to wish him a Merry Christmas and ask about Caroline Hoffman. He picked up on the first ring and assured her that Mrs. Hoffman was doing just fine. Some stitches and a concussion—and one doozy of a hangover. The hospital kept her overnight and released her earlier this afternoon. Her husband was waiting to drive her home.

The phone call started the shift in Gwendy's mood— she could still picture the dark angry gash on the woman's forehead; the glassy, excited stares of the partygoers gathered around her—and then when she stumbled upon the tattered deck of playing cards Ryan left behind, the downward spiral began in earnest.

On their second official date, many years ago in downtown

Portland, Ryan confided in her that he'd always wanted to be a magician. Gwendy was charmed by the thought and implored him to show her a magic trick. After dinner, and much convincing on Gwendy's part, they stopped at a drug store and picked up a pack of Bicycle playing cards. The two then sat on a bench in the park and Ryan demonstrated three or four different tricks, each one more elaborate than the last. Gwendy was impressed with his skills, but it was much more than that. It was *deeper* than that. This childlike wonder was a part of Ryan she'd never known existed when they were just friends, a part of his true self. That was the first time Gwendy thought: *I might be falling in love with this guy.*

Twenty minutes earlier, when Gwendy bent over to pick up her bookmark and discovered the old pack of cards sitting in a nest of dust bunnies underneath the corner of the sofa, her first reaction was one of calm gratitude: *Hey, I'm glad I found you, Ryan will be looking for you when he gets home.*

And then those four words exploded inside her head: *WHEN HE GETS HOME!*

Oh my God, he forgot his damn cards, she thought, her stomach roiling. *He never went anywhere without taking them with him. He says they're his good luck charm. He says they remind him of home and keep him safe.*

Gwendy picks up her book from the coffee table, and then immediately puts it down again. She can't focus. She glances at the television screen, jiggling her foot with nervous tension. "If he's not going to call, at least let there be something on the news. Anything. Please." She knows she talks to herself too much, but she doesn't care. No one is around to hear her.

She turns her head and stares at the button box. "What are you looking at?"

RICHARD CHIZMAR

Leaning forward, she runs her finger along the rounded edge of the wooden box, keeping a fair distance from the buttons. "You made me hurt that woman last night, didn't you?"

She feels *something* then, a slight vibration in her fingertip, and pulls her hand back. Before she realizes what she's saying: "What's that? You can help me get Ryan home?"

Sure, she thinks hazily. *Find out from the news where the rebel forces are located in Timor. Once you've pinpointed their location, push the red button. Once they're gone, the uprising's over, and Ryan comes home again. Simple.*

Gwendy shakes her head. Blinks her eyes. The room feels like it's swaying, ever so slightly, like she's riding on a ship in uneasy seas.

And, hey, while you're at it, why not do something about that jerk-off president of yours, too?

Is she thinking these thoughts or *listening* to them? It's suddenly hard to tell. "Destroy North Korea?" she asks dimly.

You need to be careful there. You do that and someone will most likely assume the U.S. military's responsible. Someone like China, let's say, and they'll want to retaliate, won't they?

"Then what are you proposing?" Her voice sounds very distant.

Not proposing anything, dear woman, just food for thought is all. But what if that president of yours were to up and disappear? Now that's not such a bad idea, huh? And just think, it's only a red button away.

Gwendy leans forward again, her eyes fixed on something far away. "Murder in the name of peace?"

You could certainly call it that, couldn't you? Personally, I rather think of it along the lines of that age-old question: if it were possible, would you travel back in time and assassinate Hitler?

Gwendy reaches out with both hands and picks up the

button box. "Richard Hamlin's a lot of things, most of them bad, but he's no Adolf Hitler."

Not yet, anyway.

She places the box in her lap and leans back into the sofa cushion. "Tempting, but who's to say the vice president will be any better. Guy's a certified fruitcake."

Then why not get rid of the lot of them? Start over fresh.

Staring at the rows of colored buttons. "I don't know . . . that's a lot to think about."

Okay then. Perhaps it would be easier to start with something . . . less far-reaching. A bitch-cow of a woman named Caroline Hoffman? How about a certain ill-mannered congressman from the state of Mississippi?

"Maybe . . ." Gwendy slowly reaches out with her right hand—

And that's when the phone rings.

50

GWENDY SHOVES THE BUTTON box off her lap and onto the sofa. Snatches up her cellphone. "Hello? Ryan? Hello?"

"I'm sorry, Mrs. Peterson," a quiet voice says. "It's Bea. Bea Whiteley."

"Bea?" she says absently. It feels like the room swims back into focus, although she can't for the life of her remember it appearing out of focus in the first place. "Is everything okay?"

"Everything's fine. I just wanted to . . . first, I want to apologize for calling so late on Christmas. I didn't even think about the three-hour time difference until the phone started ringing."

"No need to apologize, Bea. I'm wide awake."

"It sounds like Ryan didn't make it home."

Gwendy settles back into the sofa. She glances at the button box and then quickly looks away. "No, he didn't. I'm hoping to hear from him soon, though."

"I'm sorry."

"Thank you." She can hear laughter in the background. "Sounds like your grandchildren are having a Merry Christmas."

"Running around here like a bunch of wild animals."

Gwendy laughs.

"Mrs. Peterson, I called to thank you."

"For?"

"The beautiful notes you wrote inside your books to my

children. Nobody's ever said those kinds of things about me before, except for maybe my own family. I just wanted to tell you how much it meant to me."

"It was my pleasure, Bea. I meant every word."

"It was such a surprise," Bea says, sniffling. "I swear I've never seen my daughter look at me the way she did today. Like she was so proud of me."

"She has every right to be proud," Gwendy says, smiling. "Her mother's an amazing woman."

"Well, thank you again so much. I . . ." She hesitates.

"Is there something else?"

When Bea Whiteley speaks again, her voice sounds odd and tentative. "I was wondering . . . is everything else there okay, Mrs. Peterson?"

"Everything's fine," she says, sitting up and glancing at the button box again. "Why do you ask?"

"I feel silly saying it out loud, but . . . just before I called, I couldn't shake the feeling that something was wrong . . . that you were in some kind of trouble."

A shiver passes through Gwendy. "Nope, everything's fine. I've just been sitting here watching television."

"Okay . . . good." She sounds genuinely relieved. "I'll let you be now. Merry Christmas, Mrs. Peterson, and thank you again."

"Merry Christmas, Bea. I'll see you in a couple of weeks."

51

GWENDY WAKES UP EARLY the next morning with what feels like a mild hangover, despite having not touched a drop of alcohol the night before. She downs a bottle of water and knocks out a hundred sit-ups and fifty push-ups on the bedroom floor, hoping to get her blood pumping and chase away the headache. She'd slept restlessly, with unremembered dreams lurking just below her consciousness—but even without the details, she senses they were unpleasant and frightening.

The snow stopped falling a short time before daylight, leaving behind four or five inches in Castle County and most of western Maine. The traffic man on Channel Five warns travelers looking for a post-Christmas getaway to adjust their schedules for delays. Gwendy calls her father and informs him that she's coming over to shovel the driveway and sidewalk, and she's not taking no for an answer. Surprisingly, he agrees without an argument and tells her he'll have hot coffee and leftover sausage-and-egg casserole from yesterday's brunch waiting for her on the table when she arrives.

Gwendy throws on warm clothes and laces up her boots, then heads downstairs to clean off her car. Once she's finished scraping the windows and brushing off the roof, she climbs inside the Subaru and immediately turns down the heat. She's already sweating.

On her way down the hill, she spots a group of children having a snowball fight at the Castle View Rec Park. She can hear their excited shouts and squeals of delight even with the windows up. She smiles and tries to remember how long it's been since she's plunked someone with a snowball. Too long, she decides.

Ten minutes later, she turns onto Carbine Street and spots the flashing red and yellow lights of an ambulance in the distance. Her first pang of concern is for Mrs. Goff—she suffers from occasional bouts of vertigo and has fallen before. Last spring, she'd spent two weeks in the hospital nursing a broken hip. As she gets closer, Gwendy realizes the ambulance is parked in her parents' driveway and someone on a stretcher is being loaded into the back. She stomps on the brakes and fishtails to the curb.

Her father stumbles out the front door of the house, carrying Mrs. Peterson's purse in one hand and a jacket in the other. His face is drawn and pale.

"Dad!" Gwendy shouts, jumping out of the car and meeting him on the snow-covered sidewalk. "What happened? Is Mom okay?"

They both turn and watch as the ambulance pulls away, disappearing down the street.

"I don't know," he says weakly. "She started having cramps shortly after I talked to you. At first, she thought it was because she ate too much last night, but then the pain got worse. She was curled up in a ball on the bed, crying. I was about to call you when she started vomiting blood. That's when I called the ambulance. I didn't know what else to do."

Gwendy takes her father by the arm. "You did the right thing. Are they taking her to Castle County General?"

He nods, his eyes big and ready to fill with tears.

"Come on," she says, guiding him toward the curb. "I'll drive you."

141

52

THERE ARE ONLY A handful of other people sitting on the bright orange, plastic-molded seats outside of the emergency room at 10:00 AM. An older bald man nursing a sore neck from a fender-bender earlier that morning, a teenage boy with a deep cut on his lip and another under his swollen and darkening right eye from a sledding mishap, and a young Asian couple holding a pair of fussing, pink-faced twins on their laps.

When Mr. Peterson sees his wife's oncologist, Doctor Celano, emerge via the swinging doors marked NO ENTRANCE, he immediately gets to his feet and meets him in the middle of the waiting room. Gwendy scrambles to catch up.

"How is she, Doc?" he asks.

"We gave her some pain medication, so she's resting comfortably. There's been no more vomiting since the ambulance."

"Do you know what's wrong?" Gwendy asks.

"I'm afraid her tumor markers are up again," the doctor says, a solemn expression coming over his face.

"Oh, Jesus," Mr. Peterson says, sagging into his daughter's shoulder.

"I know it's difficult, but try not to get too alarmed, Mr. Peterson. Her blood tests from Wednesday's appointment just came back this morning. I pulled them up on the computer when I heard the ambulance call, and they're showing an uncomfortable increase—"

"An uncomfortable increase?" Mr. Peterson says. "What does that mean?"

"It means that most likely the cancer has returned. To what extent, we don't know yet. We're going to admit her today and run a series of tests."

"What kind of tests?" Gwendy asks.

"We've already drawn more blood this morning. Once she's settled into a room, we'll schedule abdominal and chest scans."

"Tonight?" Mr. Peterson asks.

He shakes his head. "Not on a Sunday, no. We'll let her get some rest and wheel her over to Imaging in the morning."

Mr. Peterson looks past the doctor to the swinging doors. "Can we see her?"

"Soon," Doctor Celano says. "They're transporting her to the second floor anytime now. Once she's in her room, I'll come back down and get you myself."

"Does she know yet?" Gwendy asks.

The doctor nods. "She asked me to be honest with her. I believe her exact words were: 'Do not blow sunshine up my rear. Give it to me straight.'"

Mr. Peterson shakes his head, eyes shiny with tears. "That sounds like my girl."

"Your girl's a fighter," Doctor Celano says. "So try to be as strong for her as you can. She'll need you. The both of you."

53

GWENDY OPENS THE DOOR to the house she grew up in, the only real honest-to-God house she's ever lived in—with an actual garage and sidewalk and yard—and walks inside. The interior is dark and silent. She immediately turns on the overhead light in the foyer. Her father's car keys lie on the hardwood floor, dropped in panic and unnoticed. She picks them up and returns them to their spot on the foyer table. Walking into the living room, she turns on the lamps at each end of the sofa. *That's better*, she decides. Everything looks to be in its proper place. You would never even know by looking around what kind of chaos the morning had brought.

She walks upstairs, running her hand along the polished wood bannister where four empty red stockings hang. Halfway down the carpeted hallway, she glances into her parents' bedroom, and that's when any semblance of normalcy inside the house is shattered into a million jagged pieces. The bed sheet and blankets are pushed into a heap on the floor. One of the pillows and a significant portion of the white mattress sheet are streaked with dark splashes of blood and bitesized chunks of a half-digested meal. Her father's pajamas lie in a pile on the floor at the entrance to the small walk-in closet. The entire room smells sour, like food that has been left in the sun too long and gone bad.

Gwendy stands in the doorway, taking it all in, and then she springs into action. She makes quick work of the bed, stripping the sheets, blankets, and pillowcases. Bundling them together with her father's discarded pajamas, she runs them to the basement, holding her breath, and dumps the dirty sheets and PJs into the washer. Once that's done, she returns upstairs and sprays the bedroom with a can of scented air-freshener she finds in the bathroom. Then she takes down clean sheets and pillowcases from the top shelf of the closet and remakes the bed.

Standing back and examining her work, she remembers the reason she came to the house in the first place. She finds an overnight bag and packs a change of clothes for her father, a clean nightgown for her mother, and several pairs of socks. She doesn't know why she adds the extra socks, but she figures better safe than sorry. Next she goes into the bathroom and gathers toiletries. Adding them to the bag, she zips it up tight and heads into the hallway.

Something—a feeling, a memory, she's not really sure—makes her stop outside the doorway to her old bedroom. She peers inside. Although it's long been converted into a combination guest room and sewing room, Gwendy can still picture her childhood bedroom with crystal clarity. Her beloved vanity stood against that wall, her desk, where she wrote her first stories, in front of the window. Her bookshelf right there next to a Partridge Family trashcan, her bed against the wall over there, beneath her favorite Billy Joel poster. She leans into the room and gazes at the long, narrow closet where her mother now stores swathes of cloth and sewing supplies. The same closet where she hid the button box all those years. The same closet where the first boy she ever loved had died violently right in front of her eyes, his head bashed to a bloody pulp by that monster Frankie Stone.

And that cursed box.

"What do you want from me?" she asks suddenly, her voice strained and harsh. She walks farther into the room, turns in a slow circle. "I did what you asked and I was just a goddamn child! So why are you back again!" She's shouting now, her face twisted into an angry mask. "Why don't you show yourself and stop playing games?"

The house responds with silence.

"Why me?" she whispers to the empty room.

54

MONDAYS ARE NOTORIOUSLY BUSY days at Castle County General Hospital, and December 27 is no exception. The nurses and orderlies are understaffed by nearly ten percent thanks to the holiday weekend and three members of the custodial crew call out sick because of the flu—but life marches on around here.

Gwendy sits alongside the bed in Room 233 and watches the steady rise and fall of her mother's chest. She's been sleeping peacefully for nearly a half-hour now, which is the only reason Gwendy's alone in the room with her. Twenty minutes earlier, she finally managed to shoo her father into the hallway and downstairs to the cafeteria to get himself breakfast. He hadn't left his wife's side since they were reunited yesterday afternoon and was hesitant to go, but Gwendy insisted.

The John Grisham novel sits unopened on Gwendy's lap, a coupon for granola bars marking her page. She listens to the intermittent beeping of the machines and watches the constant drip of saline and remembers dozens of other hospital rooms very much like this one. The windowless third-floor room at Mercy Hospital where her dear friend Johnathon had taken his final breaths, dozens of photographs and homemade get-well cards affixed to the wall above his head. So many other rooms in so many other hospitals and AIDS clinics she'd once visited. So many brave human beings, young and old, male and female, all united by one basic purpose: survival.

147

Ever since those days, Gwendy has loathed hospitals—the sights, smells, sounds—all while maintaining the utmost respect for those who fight for their lives there, and the doctors and nurses who aid them in that fight.

"*. . . you will die surrounded by friends, in a pretty nightgown with blue flowers on the hem. There will be sun shining in your window, and before you pass you will look out and see a squadron of birds flying south. A final image of the world's beauty. There will be a little pain. Not much.*"

Richard Farris once spoke those words to her, and she believes them to be true. She doesn't know when it will happen, or where, but that doesn't matter to her. Not anymore.

"If anyone deserves that kind of a goodbye, it's you, Mom." She looks down at her lap, stifling a sob. "But I'm not ready yet. I'm not ready."

Mrs. Peterson, eyes still closed, chest still rising and falling, says: "Don't worry, Gwennie, I'm not ready either."

"Oh my God," Gwendy almost screams in surprise, her book tumbling from her lap to the floor. "I thought you were sleeping!"

Mrs. Peterson half-opens her eyes and smiles lazily. "I was until I heard you going on and on."

"I am *so* sorry, Mom. I've been doing that, talking out loud to myself, like some kind of crazy old cat lady."

"You're allergic to cats, Gwendy," Mrs. Peterson says, matter-of-factly.

Gwendy looks closely at her mom. "Oh-kay, and that must be the morphine talking."

Mrs. Peterson lifts her head and looks around the room. "You actually convinced your father to go home?"

"Not a chance. But I did make him go to the cafeteria and get something to eat."

She nods weakly. "Good job, honey. I'm worried about him."

"I'll take care of Dad," Gwendy says. "You just worry about getting better."

"That's in God's hands now. I'm so tired."

"You can't give up, Mom. We don't even know how bad it is. It could be—"

"Who said anything about giving up? That's not going to happen, not as long as I have you and your father by my side. I have too much to live for."

"Yes," Gwendy says, nodding. "You sure do."

"All I meant is . . ." She searches for the right words. "If I'm supposed to beat this thing again, if there's any chance at all, then I'll beat it. I believe that. No matter how hard of a fight awaits me. But . . . if I'm *not* supposed to . . . if God decides this is my time, then so be it. I've lived a wonderful life with more blessings than any one person should possess. How can I possibly complain? Anyway, that's all I meant . . . that's the only way they're going to stuff me in the ground."

"Mom!" Gwendy exclaims.

"What? You know I don't want to be cremated."

"You're impossible," Gwendy says, taking down her backpack from the windowsill. "I brought you some of those little fruit juices you like so much and some snacks. Also brought you a surprise."

"Oh, goodie, I like surprises."

She unzips her backpack. "Eat and drink first, then the surprise."

"When did you get so bossy?"

"Learned from the best," Gwendy says and sticks out her tongue.

"Speaking of surprises—and I don't know why in the

149

world I woke up thinking about this just now—but do you remember the year we tried to surprise your father for his birthday?" She scoots herself up in bed, eyes wide open and alert now, and takes a sip from the small carton of juice.

"When we decorated the garage with all those balloons and streamers?" Gwendy asks.

Mrs. Peterson points a finger at her. "That's the one. He was away fishing all afternoon. We crammed everyone inside and the big plan was to hit the door opener as soon as he pulled into the driveway."

Gwendy starts giggling. "Only we didn't know he'd fallen off a log and landed in the mud on the way back to his truck."

Mrs. Peterson nods. "We'd swiped the automatic door opener from his truck so he'd had no choice but to get out." Now she's chuckling right along with her daughter.

"We were all hiding in the dark and when we heard the truck pull up and the driver's door open and close . . ."

"I hit the button and up goes the garage door and there's your father . . ." Mrs. Peterson starts laughing and can't finish.

"Standing there with his fishing pole in one hand and his tackle box in the other," Gwendy says, "and he's naked as a jaybird from the waist down, those pale skinny legs of his caked with mud." Gwendy throws her head back and laughs.

Mrs. Peterson places a hand over her heart and struggles to get the words out. "I'm covering your eyes with one hand and waving your father back to his truck with the other. I look over and see the expression on poor Blanche Goff's face . . ." She snorts out a giggle. "I thought she was going to have a heart attack sitting right there in her lawn chair."

And then both women are clutching their sides and howling with laughter—and neither one of them is able to get another word out.

55

WHEN MR. PETERSON WALKS out of the elevator and hears raucous laughter coming from somewhere down the hallway, his eyes narrow with annoyance. *Whoever's making all that racket better not wake up my wife or there's going to be hell to pay.*

It's not until he turns the corner by the nurses' station and sees the door to Room 233 standing wide open with a cluster of smiling nurses gathered outside that he realizes it's his wife and daughter making the racket.

"What's going on in here?" he asks, walking into the room with a puzzled expression on his face.

Mrs. Peterson and Gwendy take one look at him—and burst out in another fit of laughter.

56

TWENTY MINUTES LATER, AN orderly raps on the door. He's a big fellow with a warm smile and a thicket of dreadlocks crammed into a bursting-at-the-seams hairnet. "Sorry to break up the party, folks, but I'm here to take Mrs. Peterson down to Imaging."

"Winston!" Mrs. Peterson says, her face lighting up. "I thought your shift was over."

"No, ma'am." He shakes his head. "Not until I'm finished taking care of my favorite patient."

Visibly touched, she says, "Thank you, Winston."

"I'll be right here when you get back," Mr. Peterson says, squeezing his wife's hand.

She looks up at him with those beautiful blue eyes of hers and gives him a little squeeze back. "I'm ready," she says to the orderly.

"I'll be here, too," Gwendy says, doing her best not to cry.

"I know you will." Mrs. Peterson pulls her other hand out from underneath the blanket and holds up a small white feather. Her hand looks very thin and delicate. "Thanks again for the loan, sweetheart. I'll take good care of it."

Gwendy smiles, but doesn't risk saying another word.

57

BACK HOME, GWENDY SLIDES the button box into the safe and pushes the heavy door shut behind it, listening for the audible *click* as the lock engages. Then she spins the dial, once, twice, three times, and gives the handle a good hard yank just to make sure. She's almost to her bedroom when the doorbell rings.

Freezing in the hallway, she holds her breath, willing whomever it is to go away.

The doorbell rings again. A double-ring this time.

Gwendy, still dressed in the clothes she'd worn to the hospital earlier, pulls her cellphone out of her sweater pocket. She punches in 9-1-1 and hovers her finger over the SEND button. Creeping down the hallway, she eases into the foyer, careful not to make any noise, and peeks out the peephole.

The doorbell rings again—and she almost screams.

Stepping back, she unlocks the deadbolt and swings the door open.

"Jesus, Sheriff. You could have called before you—"

"Another girl's gone missing. Right down the road from here."

"What? When?"

"Call came in about an hour ago." Sheriff Ridgewick reaches down to his belt and adjusts the volume on his radio. "The girl's father said she was ice skating at the pond with friends. Some of the older kids had a bonfire going and maybe twenty-five or thirty people were there. Another parent was supposed to be watching her, but she got to talking with a neighbor, and you know how that goes. No one noticed the girl was missing until it was time to go."

"Your men checked the ice?" Gwendy asks, knowing it's a dumb question even before it leaves her mouth.

"We did," he says, nodding. "But it's been solid for at least six weeks now. No way she fell in."

"So now what? You search the area—and what else?"

"I've got officers combing the surrounding woods and side streets. We also set up roadblocks in a couple of locations, but if whoever took her stuffed her in the trunk and started driving right away, they're long gone by now. The rest of my people are knocking on doors up and down View Drive, asking folks if they've seen anything suspicious the past few days."

Gwendy's face drops. "I think you better come in, Sheriff." She takes a step back to give him room. "I have something I need to tell you, and I don't think you're going to like it."

58

THE BLONDE REPORTER FROM Channel Five holds the microphone in front of Sheriff Ridgewick's face as he speaks. She's wearing a fluffy light blue winter beanie that matches her coat and her make-up is perfect, despite the whipping wind and freezing cold temperature. The sheriff, eyes watering and cheeks raw, looks tired and miserable.

". . . is currently underway for Deborah Parker, a resident of the nineteen-hundred block of View Drive. Miss Parker is fourteen years old and a freshman at Castle Rock High School."

A color photograph of a smiling teenage girl with metal braces and dark brown curly hair appears in the upper right-hand corner of the television screen.

"She's five-foot-two-inches tall, weighs one hundred and five pounds, and has brown hair and brown eyes. She was last seen earlier this evening at approximately 7:30 PM. ice skating with friends at Fortier Pond. If anyone has any information as to Deborah Parker's whereabouts or witnessed anything out of the ordinary in the Castle View area, please contact the Castle Rock Sheriff's Department at . . ."

59

GWENDY HAS NEVER LAID eyes on the man standing outside of the sheriff's office before, but she can smell his press credentials a mile away. It also helps that she can see the mini-recorder he's palming in his left hand.

"Congresswoman Peterson," he says, cutting her off by the entrance. "Any comment on the missing girls?"

"And you are?" she asks.

He pulls a laminated ID card out from under his jacket and extends it as far as the lanyard will permit. "Ronald Blum, *Portland Press Herald*."

"I'm here this morning to be briefed by Sheriff Ridgewick. I'll leave it to him to issue any official statements." She starts to walk away.

"Is it true that there've been other unsuccessful recent attempts to abduct young girls here in Castle Rock?"

Gwendy pulls opens the door and lets it swing closed in the reporter's face. He shouts something else, but she can't make it out through the heavy glass.

The stationhouse is buzzing this morning. A handful of officers sit at their desks talking on the telephone and jotting down notes. Several others are gathered in front of a bulletin board, examining a large map of Castle Rock. There's a line at the coffee machine and another in front of the Xerox copier. Gwendy spots Sheila Brigham in her cubicle and heads that way.

The veteran dispatcher is busy talking to someone on her headset, and judging by the annoyed look on her face, she's been stuck on the line for quite some time. She sees Gwendy approach and covers the microphone with her hand. "Go on back. It's a shit-show here today."

Gwendy waves thank you and walks down the narrow hallway. This time the door to Sheriff Ridgewick's office is closed. She knocks three times for luck.

"Come in," a muffled voice says.

She opens the door and steps inside. The sheriff is standing at the window, staring outside. "That reporter get you on the way in?"

She nods. "I didn't have much to say."

"I appreciate that," he says, turning around and looking at her.

"He asked if there'd been any other attempted abductions in Castle Rock recently. I almost fainted, but I don't think he noticed."

"He's just fishing," the sheriff says, leaning back against his desk.

"I guess, but it was very unsettling after what I told you last night."

"He doesn't know anything about that. Nobody does. Yet."

"You'll tell the others today?"

He nods. "The State Police are sending additional detectives later this morning. We're setting up a task force, so I'll be sharing your story during the initial briefing."

"Let me know if you need me to be there to face the music in person."

"That won't be necessary," he says almost casually. "What I'll say is, you thought the whole thing was a prank until you got to thinking about it later on. That's when you realized that maybe the guy had been wearing a mask. So you told me all about it this morning. You didn't see a vehicle and are unable to provide a physical description of the man other than dark clothes and shoes with some sort of a heel."

She looks at him with gratitude. "Thank you, Norris."

"Don't mention it," he says, waving her off. "No need for the whole damn world to discover how hard-headed you are."

Gwendy laughs. "Now you sound like my mother."

60

WHEN GWENDY WALKS INTO Room 233 on the second floor
of Castle County General and sees the tears streaming down
both her mother and father's faces, her heart drops.

Mrs. Peterson is sitting on the edge of the hospital bed
with her bare legs dangling over the side. She's holding hands
with her husband and leaning her head against his shoulder.
She looks very much like a young girl. Doctor Celano stands
at the foot of the bed, reading from an open chart. When he
hears the door open, he turns to Gwendy with a big, toothy
grin on his face.

"I'm sorry I'm late," Gwendy says, confused. "I got held
up in a meeting."

Her father looks up at her. His eyes are watery and dancing and he's also wearing a broad smile.

"What's going on?" Gwendy asks, feeling like she just
stepped into the Twilight Zone.

"Oh, honey, it's a miracle," her mother says, holding out
her arms.

Gwendy goes to her and gives her a hug. "What is? What's
happening?" Her mother only squeezes tighter.

Mr. Peterson nods to the doctor. "Tell her what you just
told us."

Doctor Celano raises his eyebrows. "All of the scans came
back clean. No sign of a tumor anywhere."

"What? That's great news, right?" Gwendy asks, afraid to get her hopes up.

"I'd say so."

"But what about the blood results?"

The doctor waves the medical chart at her. "The blood work we took yesterday morning also came back clean. Your mother's numbers are squarely in the normal range."

"How is that possible?" Gwendy asks in disbelief.

"I wondered the same thing myself," Doctor Celano says, "so I put in a request right away for additional blood work and rushed the lab for the results."

"I was curious what was going on," Mrs. Peterson says, laughing. "They took three more tubes before breakfast, and I told the nurse she was turning into a vampire."

"The new tests came back normal. Again," the doctor says, closing the chart and holding it at his side.

Gwendy stares at him. "Could it be a mistake?"

"A mistake was made, but not yesterday or today. I'm positive these results are accurate." The doctor sighs heavily and the smile disappears from his face. "With that said, I want to assure you that I'll get to the bottom of what went wrong in regards to Mrs. Peterson's initial blood work on the 22nd. It was a reprehensible error, and I *will* find out where it occurred."

"But what about the stomach pain? The vomiting?"

"That's a bit of a mystery, I'm afraid," the doctor says. "My best guess is she ate something that didn't agree with her and the force of the vomiting agitated scar tissue that was caused by the chemotherapy. It's happened to patients of mine before."

"So what . . . what does this all mean?" Gwendy asks.

"It means she's not sick!" Mr. Peterson says, putting an

arm around Gwendy's shoulder and giving her a shake. "It means we can take her home!"

"Today?" Gwendy says, looking at the doctor. She still can't believe this is happening. "Right now?"

"As soon as we're finished with her discharge papers."

Gwendy gazes at Doctor Celano for a moment, and then looks back at her parents. Their faces are alight with happiness. "I'm starting to think that feather of yours really is magic," her father says.

And then all three of them are laughing again and holding on to each other for dear life.

61

In most of eastern Maine, news of an approaching nor'easter—still four or five days out but already gaining strength at a monstrous rate—fills the airwaves and front pages of newspapers over the next forty-eight hours. There's very little panic in this part of the world, even when it comes to the bigger storms—but there *is* an underlying sense of dread. Blizzards mean accidents—both on the roads and closer to home. There will be broken bones and frostbite; overturned cars in ditches and downed power lines. Elderly folks will be rendered housebound, unable to venture out to grocery stores and pharmacies; meals and refills will be missed and illnesses will slither under drafty door cracks with insidious stealth and take hold. The youngsters won't fare much better, as they gleefully abandon whatever common sense they possess in the first place to rush headlong outside into the storm to build forts and wage snowball wars and hurtle down tree-speckled hills at breakneck speeds on flimsy slivers of drugstore plastic. If town folks are lucky, no one will need a mortician. But then again nor'easters aren't usually harbingers of anything even close to resembling good luck.

This time, in the western half of the state, it's a different story altogether. The approaching blizzard is relegated to page two or even three, and only discussed in detail during the weather portion of most television newscasts. The three missing Castle County girls dominate local media coverage from early morning drive-time to the eleven o'clock nightly news. Family members and friends, schoolmates and even teachers are interviewed, all offering a slightly modified version of the same somber story: the three girls are kind and talented and have never been in any kind of trouble; they certainly didn't run away from home. Sheriff Norris Ridgewick and State Police Detective Frank Thome are also constant on-air presences. They continue to offer the same grim-faced reassurances that their respective departments are doing everything humanly possible to locate the missing girls and the same passionate requests for information from the public. Their singular message and lack of originality in delivering that message prompts one local reporter to write that both men "are reading from the same uninspired script."

Despite the lack of recovered bodies or anything else resembling proof, the Portland press have already begun to throw around the "serial killer" moniker and have dredged up no fewer than three sidebar articles relating to Frank Dodd and his stint as "The Castle Rock Strangler" in the early 1970s.

In Castle Rock, there are no mentions of Boogeyman Dodd in the press—although there are plenty of whispers in the bars and restaurants and stores; in a small town like The Rock, the whispering never ends. The December 30, 1999 edition of *The Castle Rock Call* features large photos of each of the three girls above the front-page fold and a banner headline running just below that reads: MANHUNT TURNS UP NO CLUES – TASK FORCE PUZZLED.

Gwendy Peterson takes one look at the newspaper and tosses it unread onto her parents' dining-room table. "Let's go, slowpokes!" she yells upstairs. "We're going to be late!"

Gwendy and her father have spent the past two days

taking excellent care of Mrs. Peterson—at least that's what they would claim if asked. Mrs. Peterson, on the other hand, would tell a completely different story; without hesitation or filter, she'd tell you they've spent the past two days driving her bat-shit crazy.

Despite the doctor's words of assurance—both at the hospital and during a follow-up phone call yesterday afternoon—Mr. Peterson insisted that his wife remain on the family-room sofa for the remainder of the week, resting and recovering under a pile of blankets.

"Recovering from what?" Mrs. Peterson retorted. "I ate something bad and puked. Big deal. End of story."

For once, Gwendy took her father's side of the argument, and the two of them wore a path in the carpet leading to and from the sofa, trying to make sure she was comfortable and adequately entertained. In the process, they also wore out Mrs. Peterson's patience. After two days spent reading a half-dozen magazines from cover to cover, watching hours of television, knitting, and working on another jigsaw puzzle until she was seeing double, Mrs. Peterson finally lost it, shortly after lunch, hurling the television remote at her husband and declaring, "Stop babying me, dammit! I feel fine!"

And it seems like she really does. Only one short nap yesterday, and nothing at all so far today. The color has returned to her face and her appetite—as well as her spunky attitude—is back to normal. In fact, a short time ago, she not so subtly hinted (insisted) that Gwendy and Mr. Peterson take her out to dinner tonight, and not just any old restaurant, either. She has Gwendy call her favorite Italian bistro, Giovanni's, in neighboring Windham, and make a reservation for three (which they'll be late for if they don't leave the house in the next few minutes).

Gwendy turns at the sound of footsteps and can't believe her eyes. "Wow," she says, getting up from the table. "You look like a million bucks, Mom."

"A billion," a smiling Mr. Peterson says, coming down the stairs behind her.

Mrs. Peterson is wearing a dark blue dress underneath a long gray sweater. For the first time in months, she has on lipstick and eye shadow. Gold earrings dangle from her ears and a single pearl necklace hangs around her neck.

"Thank you," Mrs. Peterson says primly. "If you keep up the compliments, I will consider forgiving the both of you."

"In that case," Mr. Peterson says, extending his arm toward the front door, "your chariot awaits."

62

THE DRIVE FROM CASTLE Rock to Windham takes forty-five minutes but dinner is worth every mile of it. Both Gwendy and Mrs. Peterson order stuffed shrimp a la Guiseppi, side salads, and cups of seafood bisque. Mr. Peterson decides on chicken cacciatore and devours an entire loaf of Italian bread all by himself before his entrée arrives. "You keep that up," Mrs. Peterson tells him, "and we'll be visiting *you* in the hospital."

After they finish eating, Mr. and Mrs. Peterson take to the dance floor and slow dance to back-to-back ballads sung by a Frank Sinatra look-alike set up on a small stage by the bar. At the conclusion of the last song, Mr. Peterson dips his wife over his bended knee, before pulling her close for a kiss on the cheek. They return to the table giggling like a couple of high-school sweethearts.

"You sure you don't want to give it a whirl, Gwennie?" her father asks, sliding out Mrs. Peterson's chair for her. "I still have a little gas left in the tank."

"I'm stuffed. I think I'll just sit here until I float away."

"Will there be dessert for anyone?" the waitress says from over Mrs. Peterson's shoulder.

"Not me," Gwendy says, groaning.

Mr. Peterson pats his full belly. "None for me, either."

"No, thank you, dear," Mrs. Peterson says, and as her husband asks the waitress for the check, she turns to Gwendy. "I think I'll just have one of those yummy chocolates of yours when I get home instead."

63

GWENDY JOGS UP THE last hilly stretch of Pleasant Road, sticking as close to the shoulder as she can. After two close calls this morning, she's especially wary of the increased traffic, even at such an early hour. It's been three long days since fourteen-year-old Deborah Parker disappeared from Fortier Pond, but the neighborhood is still bustling with a combination of police and sheriff vehicles, volunteer searchers, and curious lookie-loos, mostly out-of-towners with their noses pressed against the glass of their windshields.

Gwendy's schedule on this chilly final day of the twentieth century is remarkably clear (a fact she grudgingly attributes to a lack of anything resembling a healthy social life). After she finishes her run and showers, she plans to catch up on some overdue email correspondence, then swing by her parents' house for a quick check-in—Mr. and Mrs. Peterson are going next door to the Goff's later this evening for dinner—and then it's back home for an exciting afternoon of John Grisham before it's finally time to leave for Brigette Desjardin's PTA New Year's Eve party. She's already prepared a five-minute speech for the occasion and is hoping she doesn't have to stick around for much longer than that.

As she turns the corner and her building comes into view, Gwendy's thoughts turn to the button box and the miniature chocolate animals.

So far, she's given her mom a total of seven pieces of

chocolate—the first one a tiny turtle she smuggled into the hospital along with several cartons of fruit juice, and the most recent an adorable little pig when they got home from the restaurant last night.

Before pulling the lever on the left side of the box and slipping the bite-sized chocolate turtle into a sandwich bag and stuffing it into the zippered pocket of her backpack to take to the hospital, Gwendy agonized long and hard over the decision. She knew from firsthand experience that the button box dispensed not-so-tiny doses of magic along with its animal treats—but she also knew the gifts were rarely delivered without consequence. *So what exactly was going to happen the first time she gave someone else one of the chocolates? How about a whole bunch of them?* Gwendy didn't know the answers, but in the end, she was willing to roll the dice.

It wasn't until the other morning at the hospital when Doctor Celano gave them the miraculous news that she finally felt at peace with her decision. How could she not after that? But if Gwendy was holding onto any lingering doubts—and, okay, maybe there *were* just a few—it was the graceful dip at the end of that last slow dance and the dreamy look on her mother's face when Mr. Peterson planted the tender kiss on her cheek that sent those doubts packing once and for all. Gwendy knew she would remember that moment and her parents' laughter for the rest of her life (however long that might be).

Gwendy offers a cheerful good morning to her across-the-hall neighbor exiting the building and bounds up the stairs to the second floor, feeling light on her feet. She unzips her pocket and pulls out her key and cellphone. She's reaching for the doorknob when she notices the MESSAGE light blinking on her telephone.

"No, no, no," she says, realizing she forgot to turn on her ringer. She pushes the button to retrieve her messages and holds the phone up to her ear.

"Hey, honey, I can't believe I got through! Been trying for days! I miss you so—"

The message cuts off in mid-sentence.

Gwendy stares at her phone in disbelief.

"Come on . . ." She fumbles with the buttons, trying to find out if there's another message. There isn't. She hits the REPEAT button and stands in front of her door, listening to those four seconds of Ryan's voice. Over and over again.

64

GWENDY SITS CROSS-LEGGED ON the bed, wet hair wrapped in a towel, and hits SEND on the email she just finished writing. Once the modem disconnects from dial-up, she closes her laptop. A look of concern on her face, she swings her legs off the bed and starts to get dressed. She's tying her shoes when the phone rings.

"Hello?" Trying not to get her hopes up.

"Gwendy, it's Patsy Follett. I catch you at a bad time?"

"Patsy!" she says, excited to hear the congresswoman's voice. "I just responded to your email."

"And I just opened it and read it. Figured it'd be easier to call."

"Well, how are you?" Gwendy asks. "Happy New Year!"

"Happy New Year to you, too. I was doing great until I talked to my friend in the Senate this morning. Then, not so great."

"You really think we're going to be called back early?"

"That's what he said. Some kind of emergency session because of President Big Mouth and Korea. First time it's happened since Harry flippin' Truman."

"That means there's more going on behind the scenes than the news is telling us."

"Evidently," Patsy says with disgust in her voice. "I gotta admit this is the first time I've actually been scared the idiot's going to get us in another war."

Gwendy looks across the bedroom at the button box on the dresser. She walks over to it.

"I lose you, Gwen?"

"No, no, I'm right here. Just thinking."

65

GWENDY ONLY STAYS AT her parents' house for a short time that afternoon, just long enough to talk Patriots football with her dad (he thinks Pete Carroll has to go after another fourth-place finish; she believes he deserves one more year to turn things around) and help her mom pick out an outfit for the New Year's Eve dinner later that night at the Goffs.

She's already outside on the front porch digging in her coat pockets for her car keys when Mrs. Peterson swings open the door and stops her. "Hold on a second. I need to talk to you about something."

Gwendy turns around. "You need to get back inside, Mom, before you catch a cold. It's freezing out here."

"This'll only take a second."

It's bad news, Gwendy thinks, reading the expression on her face. *I knew it was too good to be true.*

"I'm afraid I have some bad news."

"Oh, Mom," Gwendy says. "What is it?"

"I should've told you before now, but I kept chickening out."

Gwendy goes to her. "Just tell me what's wrong."

"I've checked my bag, I've looked everywhere, I even called the hospital . . . but I can't find your magic feather anywhere."

Gwendy stares at her—and starts laughing.

"What?" Mrs. Peterson asks. "What's so funny?"

"I thought . . . I thought you were going to tell me you were sick again, that the hospital had made another mistake."

Mrs. Peterson places a hand over her heart. "Dear God no."

"The feather will turn up if it's supposed to," Gwendy says, opening the door. "It did once before. Now get inside, you silly woman."

66

On her way home from Carbine Street, Gwendy sees Sheriff Ridgewick's cruiser parked on the shoulder of Route 117 with its hazard lights blinking. She hits her turn signal and pulls over behind him.

As she gets out of the car, she spots the sheriff climbing out of a snowy ravine that runs alongside the highway. He's up to his hips in drifting snow and cussing up a blue streak.

"What would your constituents think if they heard you talking like that?"

The sheriff looks up at her with snow in his hair and daggers in his eyes. "They'd think I've had a shitty-ass day, which I have."

Gwendy extends a hand to help. "What were you doing down there, anyway?"

"Thought I saw something," he says, taking her hand. He pops out of the ditch and starts stomping his boots on the gravel shoulder. He looks up at her. "I was just about to call you before I pulled over."

"What's up?"

He rubs a hand over his chin. "We received a padded envelope at the stationhouse about an hour ago. No return address. Postmarked yesterday in Augusta."

Gwendy feels her face flush. She knows what's coming next.

"The orange ski hat Deborah Parker was wearing the

afternoon she went ice-skating was inside the envelope. And stuffed inside the hat . . . three more teeth, presumably hers."

Gwendy gapes at him, unable to find the words.

"To make matters worse, I just got off the phone a little while ago with that reporter from the *Portland Herald*. Someone leaked. He knows about the teeth we found in the sweatshirt and he knows about the package."

"But you said it was only delivered an hour ago."

He nods. "That's right."

"So how . . .?"

Sheriff Ridgewick shrugs. "Someone needed the money I guess. Anyway, he's working on an article for tomorrow morning's paper and he's already calling the guy 'The Tooth Fairy.'"

"Jesus."

"Ayuh," he says grimly. "Shit's about to hit the fan."

67

GWENDY'S BRIEF SPEECH AT the PTA New Year's Eve party goes over well and earns her a spirited round of applause from the audience, along with the usual smattering of catcalls. Castle Rock may be proud of its hometown-girl-made-good, but there are still plenty of folks around here who don't believe a woman should be representing their voice in the nation's capital, much less a thirty-seven-year-old woman who happens to be a Democrat. That's what many of the old-timers down at the corner store call "adding insult to injury."

When Brigette originally explained that the plan was for everyone inside the Municipal Center to file outside to Castle Rock Common at 11:00 PM so the big midnight countdown could take place in the center of town by the clock tower, Gwendy believed it was the very epitome of a bad idea. It would be dark and freezing cold. People would be tired and cranky. She predicted that most folks would probably just head for their cars and the warmth of their living rooms at that point to celebrate the ball dropping with Dick Clark and assorted celebrity guests on television.

But she was dead wrong, she admitted now.

The PTA volunteers had created quite the festive winter wonderland on the Common, hanging dozens of strings of twinkling white Christmas lights in the trees and shrubbery, around the railing and the roof of the bandstand, and along the white picket fence that bordered the woods at the northern edge of the Common. Red and green streamers hung from lampposts and street signs. A hot chocolate and coffee booth had been set up by the entrance, and someone had even dressed up the War Memorial, draping a bright red ribbon around the WWI soldier's neck and scrubbing the splatters of birdshit off his pie-dish helmet.

Conspicuous in their absence were the number of HAVE YOU SEEN THIS GIRL? posters missing from nearby tele-phone poles and lampposts and the windows of the handful of buildings that bordered the Common. For a few hours on one night only, talk of the missing girls had been pushed to the background and folks were focusing on the positive and hopeful. Tomorrow morning, the posters and the chatter would undoubtedly return.

At 11:45 PM, as Gwendy stands in line waiting for hot chocolate, the place is positively hopping. Kids dart past her in eager packs, shouting and laughing, tossing snowballs at each other and sliding on stray patches of ice, while their parents and neighbors wander around, flitting from huddled group to huddled group, chatting, gossiping, sneaking sips of whis-key from hidden flasks, and making grandiose plans for 2000 to be the best year ever. Gwendy spots Grace Featherstone from the Book Nook talking to Nanette from the diner over by the bandstand. Brigette is holding court with a number of her PTA minions by the picnic tables, no doubt making sure everything's set for midnight and the big countdown. Gwendy saw Mr. and Mrs. Hoffman earlier inside the hall, but did her best to avoid them—going so far as to hide in the bathroom for much longer than was probably necessary. So far, so good, in that regard—she hasn't seen either one of them again since.

The line inches forward, and she notices a tall man with

a bushy mustache wearing a Patriots cap leaning against a lamppost by the fountain. He appears to be watching her, but Gwendy can't be sure she isn't imagining it. She thinks she remembers seeing him earlier in the audience during her speech.

"That you, Mrs. Gwendy Peterson?"

She turns around. It takes her a second to recognize the older man standing behind her, but then it comes to her in a flash. "Well, hello again, Mr. Charlie Browne."

"Just Charlie, please."

"Enjoying the New Year's Eve festivities?"

"I was enjoying it a lot more when we were inside and I wasn't freezing my giblets off."

Gwendy tosses her head back and laughs. "Good thing the wind isn't blowing, or we'd look like a bunch of ice sculptures out here."

He grunts and looks around. "You see my boy around anywhere? That clock strikes midnight and I'm outta here."

Gwendy shakes her head. "Sorry, I haven't seen him."

"There you are," Brigette says, arriving in a perfume-scented flurry. "I was looking for you. What are you doing waiting in line?" She waves furiously at one of the women in the booth. "Can I get a hot cocoa ASAP for the congresswoman?"

"Brigette, no," Gwendy says, horrified. People are staring at them, some of them pointing.

"Here you go," a dark-haired woman says, hustling over with a steaming Styrofoam cup.

Gwendy doesn't want to accept it, but she has no choice. "Thank you. You really didn't have to do that."

"Nonsense," Brigette says, taking her by the arm and leading her away. "I want you right next to me at midnight."

"Happy New Year, Mr. Browne," Gwendy says over her shoulder. "It was nice seeing you again."

"Happy New Year, Congresswoman," he says, smirking, and Gwendy doesn't know if it's her imagination or not, but she's almost positive his tone is no longer a friendly one.

"Three more minutes," Brigette says, glancing at her watch. She spots her husband standing across the Common talking to two other men. "Travis! Travis!" She points at the clock tower. "Over there!"

He nods dutifully and starts in that direction.

The miniature clock tower is located at the very heart of the Castle Rock Common. It stands twenty-two feet high and its face measures three feet across its center. Erected during the town's reconstruction period in the aftermath of the Big Fire, there's an engraved metal plaque positioned at the stone base of the tower that reads: *In honor of the indomitable spirit of the citizens of Castle Rock — 1992.*

A burly woman wearing what looks like several layers of flannel shirts flashes a look of relief as they approach. "Thank goodness, I was starting to get worried." She hands Brigette a microphone. A long black cord snakes from the bottom of the mic to a large speaker propped up on a picnic table behind them.

Gwendy smiles at the woman. "Happy New Year."

"Happy New Year," she says shyly, and quickly looks away.

Travis walks up beside them, grinning and smelling like aftershave and whiskey. "All ready to go, ladies?"

"Almost," Brigette says. She turns on the microphone and a whine of feedback erupts from the speaker. People groan and cover their ears. The woman in the flannel shirts scurries to adjust several knobs at the top of the speaker until the sound diminishes and finally dissipates.

"One minute til midnight!" Brigette announces, giddily. "One minute until midnight!"

A crowd starts to gather at the foot of the clock tower, the younger kids swarming toward the front, most of them wearing glow-in-the-dark necklaces and carrying party horns or noisemakers. Many of the adults are wearing glittery cardboard hats with Y2K! or 2000! or HAPPY NEW YEAR! printed across the brims at jaunty angles.

"Thirty seconds!" Brigette shouts, her tone bordering on hysterical, and for the first time tonight, Gwendy wonders how much her friend has had to drink.

Studying the crowd, she sees Grace and Nanette and Milly Harris, the church organist, huddled together off to the side. All three are staring up at the clock and counting down. Charlie Browne is standing toward the back by himself with his foot propped up on a bench. He's wearing scuffed cowboy boots and a green plastic derby with a fake yellow flower poking out from the top. He grins and gives Gwendy a big wave. She gratefully waves back, thinking she must've been wrong about him before.

Maybe ten yards behind Mr. Browne is the mustached stranger in the Patriots cap. He's scanning the crowd, but it's hard to get a good look at his face because the brim of his hat is tilted so low.

"TEN, NINE, EIGHT, SEVEN, SIX . . ." Brigette lowers the microphone from her mouth. The roar of the crowd has grown louder than her amplified voice.

"FIVE . . . FOUR . . . THREE . . . TWO . . . ONE . . ."

The crowd erupts. "HAPPY NEW YEARRRR!"

A cacophony of drunken hooting and hollering, blowing horns and honking noisemakers fills the air. Confetti is tossed by the handfuls. Someone on the other side of the Common shoots off a string of bottle rockets. Brilliant explosions of red, white, and blue sparks light up the night sky and shower down upon the snow-covered ground. Everywhere around Gwendy, people are embracing and kissing. She thinks of Ryan, the way his whiskers tickle her chin when he kisses her, and a deep ache blooms in the center of her chest.

Brigette untangles herself from her husband's arms, and then it's Gwendy's turn. "Happy New Year!" she shouts above the clatter, hugging Gwendy tight. "I'm so glad you're here!"

"Happy New Year!" Gwendy says, her face awash in the glow of fireworks.

"My turn next." Travis is standing behind his wife, arms held open wide, looking at Gwendy. "Happy New Year!"

Gwendy leans over and hugs him and the side of her face brushes against the cold skin of Travis's cheek. "Happy New—" she starts to say, and then something changes.

Everything changes.

Suddenly Travis appears very clear to her, very *bright* and in focus, almost as if he's somehow lit from within, and everything else around him falls away. She notices the tiny scar on Travis's chin and immediately *understands* that the neighbor's dog, Barney, snapped at Travis when he was eight years old because he'd been throwing rocks at it from across the chain-link fence. This was in Boston, where Travis grew up. She stares at the thick, wavy texture of his hair and suddenly *understands* that he's having an affair with his hair dresser, a single woman named Katy who lives in a trailer on the outskirts of town with her three-year-old son. Her dear old friend Brigette knows nothing about it . . .

. . . and then Gwendy's vision blurs and Travis suddenly swirls out of view, like he's being sucked into the maw of a pitch-black vortex, and everything else around him swims back into focus.

"—you okay?" Travis asks. He's standing a few feet away, staring at her with concern in his eyes.

Gwendy blinks and looks around. "I'm fine," she says. "Felt a little light-headed for a minute there."

"Christ, I thought you were having a seizure or something," he says.

"Come on," Brigette says, taking her by the arm. "Let's sit down."

"Honest, I'm fine." She wants out of there, and she wants out of there right now. "I think it's time I head home. It's been a long day."

"Are you sure you should be driving? Travis could take—"

"I'm good," Gwendy says, forcing a smile. "I promise."

Brigette gives her a lingering look. "Okay, but please be careful."

"Will do," Gwendy says, waving goodbye. "I'll talk to you tomorrow."

What in the hell was that all about? she thinks, cutting across the Common on the way to her car. She doesn't even know how to describe what just happened, but she knows she's never experienced anything remotely like it before. It's almost as if a door had opened, and she'd stepped inside. But opened to what? Travis's soul? It sounded hokey, like something out of a science fiction novel, but it also made a certain amount of sense to her, the same way that the button box made a certain amount of sense to her now.

Was what happened some kind of a bizarre side effect because of the chocolates she'd given to her Mom? And why Travis? She barely knew the guy, and he certainly wasn't the only person she'd come in contact with tonight. She shook hands with dozens of other people.

A dark figure suddenly steps out of the shadows in front of her. "Are you okay, Mrs. Peterson?"

Startled, Gwendy jerks to a stop. It's the stranger in the Patriots cap, and he's standing close enough to reach out and touch her. She's trapped in between buildings now, and it's darker here without the streetlights.

"I'm fine," she says, trying to sound unafraid. "You really should be more careful about ambushing people like that. Especially with everything that's going on around here."

"I apologize," the man says in a pleasant tone. "I saw what happened and was concerned."

"You saw what happened," Gwendy repeats with an edge to her voice. "And why were you watching me in the first place, Mr. . . . ?"

"Nolan," the man says, pulling open his coat to reveal a badge clipped to his belt. "Detective Nolan."

Gwendy's eyes widen and she feels a flush spread across her cheeks. "And now I feel very foolish."

The detective holds up his hands. "Please don't, ma'am. I should have identified myself right away."

"Did Sheriff Ridgewick ask you to keep an eye on me?"

"No, ma'am," he says. "Way he talks about you, I'm pretty sure the sheriff thinks you can take care of yourself."

Gwendy laughs. She can picture Norris saying exactly those words. "Well, have a good night, detective. Thanks for checking on me."

He nods mutely and starts walking back in the direction of the Common.

Gwendy turns toward the street and, in the time it takes to recognize the man walking toward her, she decides to conduct an experiment. "Hey, there, Mr. Gallagher," she says. "Happy New Year." She tugs the glove off her right hand and extends it toward him.

"Happy New Year to you, too, young lady." Gwendy's eighth grade algebra teacher shakes her hand with a firm grip. She can feel the rough callouses on his palm. "You should stop by the school one day. The kids would love to see you."

"I'll do that," she says, waiting for something, *anything*, out of the ordinary to happen.

But it doesn't.

So she keeps walking until she reaches Main Street where she parked her car. She's thinking about the button box and its chocolate treats and not looking where she's going when her feet suddenly go out from under her. One minute she's striding confidently past the Castle Rock Diner, catching a fleeting glimpse of her reflection in the darkened front window, and the next she's skidding across an icy patch of sidewalk, her arms flailing above her head.

Someone grabs her around the waist.

"Oh my God," she says, steadying herself.

"That was a close one, Mrs. Peterson." Lucas Browne lets go of her waist and reaches down to the sidewalk. He comes back up holding her glove. "You dropped this." He smiles and hands it to her and their bare fingers touch . . .

. . . and Main Street suddenly falls away, the cars and storefronts and streetlights disappearing, and all she can see is *him*, in brilliant, almost luminescent, detail. And just like that she *knows*. Lucas Browne is the Tooth Fairy. She stares at his hand and watches as his gloved fingers wrap around a stainless steel instrument, reach into a dummy mouth full of fake teeth set up on a brightly lit table, *UB School of Dental Medicine* stitched across the breast of the long white lab coat he's wearing . . . and then those same fingers, filthy now, gripping a pair of rusty workroom pliers, and he's standing over a cowering Deborah Parker, her long hair spiked with sweat, her eyes wide and frightened, the tips of his cowboy boots splattered with fat drops of blood . . .

And then the darkness swallows him away, and the streetscape sharpens into focus again and Lucas Browne is standing on the sidewalk in front of her.

"What just happened?" he asks, eyes narrowing. "Are you okay?"

"I'm . . . I'm fine," she says. "Thank you. You saved me from a nasty fall." Her voice sounds dull and distant.

A young couple, walking arm-in-arm, passes by then. The teenage boy, a James Dean wannabe with his leather jacket and cigarette dangling from his mouth, nods at them. "What's up, Lucas?"

Lucas doesn't answer, doesn't even look at the guy—just watches Gwendy cross the street with that same wary look on his face.

Gwendy unlocks the car and climbs inside, hurriedly locking the door behind her. Her hands are shaking and her heart feels like it's going to burst inside her chest. She starts the engine and pulls away without letting it warm up. When she glances toward the sidewalk, Lucas Browne is still standing there, watching her.

68

SHERIFF RIDGEWICK PICKS UP on the first ring. "Hello?"

"It's Lucas Browne!" Gwendy nearly shouts. "Lucas Browne's the Tooth Fairy!"

"Gwendy? Do you know what time it is?"

"Listen to me, Norris. Please. I think Deborah Parker's still alive, but I don't know how much time she has."

"Okay, start over and tell me how you know this."

"I just ran into Lucas Browne on Main Street and—"

"What were you doing on Main Street at this time of night?"

"I was walking to my car after the New Year's Eve party," she says, her frustration building, "but that's not important. Lucas Browne went to dental school in Buffalo."

"How exactly do you know that? For that matter, how do you know Lucas Browne?"

"I met him and his father when we were searching the field that day. His father told me Lucas went to college in Buffalo, but he came home early after he got into some kind of trouble."

"And Lucas told you it was dental school when you saw him tonight?"

She doesn't answer right away. "Something like that." She takes a deep breath. "Norris, he was wearing cowboy boots. I think there was blood on them."

Rustling in the background now. "Where are you?"

"I just turned on 117. Headed home."

"Turn around," he says, and she can hear a door opening and closing. "Meet me at the station. Don't call anyone else."

"Hurry, Norris."

69

GWENDY PULLS UP A chair and sits next to Sheila Brigham inside the dispatch cubicle, listening to the radio calls as they come in. She recognizes Sheriff Ridgewick right away, although his voice sounds much deeper over the airwaves, and State Trooper Tom Noel, who was a year behind her at Castle Rock High and grew up two blocks away from Carbine Street. The others are strangers to her, their words terse and clipped, but Gwendy can hear the excitement simmering in their voices.

The sheriff and Deputy Footman are in the lead car, followed by a large convoy of Castle County Sheriff's Department, Castle Rock Police Department, and Maine State Police vehicles. They've just crossed over the old railroad bridge on Jessup Road and will be splitting up and surrounding the Browne's ranch house in a matter of minutes.

Despite numerous requests and a half-hearted attempt at bribery (involving one of Mr. Peterson's prized fly fishing rods), the sheriff refused to allow Gwendy to ride along with him or his men—the press would have a field day, he argued, especially if something went wrong and she were injured—so this is the closest she'll get to the action.

She stares at the radio with nervous anticipation, tapping her foot on the ugly green carpet and chewing her fingernails. Sheila has already scolded her twice for not being able to sit still, but Gwendy can't help it. She's running on fumes and nearly a half-dozen cups of coffee. It's almost ten o'clock in the morning and she hasn't slept a wink. In fact, she didn't even make it home last night.

Shortly after 1:00 AM, not long after meeting Gwendy at the stationhouse, Sheriff Ridgewick got in touch with a Detective Tipton of the Buffalo Police Department. Files were pulled. Phone calls made. Doors knocked on. By 6:00 AM, a senior official from the Administration Office at the University of Buffalo verified that Lucas Tillman Browne of Castle Rock, Maine was dismissed from the School of Dental Medicine—just before the conclusion of his third semester— after numerous female students filed sexual harassment and stalking complaints against him. Shortly after 8:00 AM, State Police detectives learned from the Tomlinsons and the Parkers that both families had hired handyman Charles Browne the previous spring to power-wash the aluminum siding on their houses. In both instances, Mr. Browne had been accompanied by his son. It'd been so long ago the families had simply forgotten. This treasure trove of new information led to a search warrant being issued for the Browne residence and the surrounding property.

"I've got eyes on a single male subject," the radio squawks, and Gwendy can picture Sheriff Ridgewick sitting in the driver's seat of his cruiser, squinting through a dirty wind-shield. *"Check that, two male subjects in the garage. Second man's working under the truck."*

"Copy that. We're in position out back."

"All good at the fence line. He comes this way, we got 'em."

"Approaching subjects now. Detective Thome is at my twelve o'clock blocking the driveway. Stand by."

Three-and-a-half minutes later: *"Warrant has been served. Both subjects cooperating. Detectives entering the residence. Stand by."*

The radio goes mostly silent then. Someone requests a new pair of gloves be brought inside the house. Another officer asks if he and his men should continue to turn away traffic at the intersection. Deputy Portman responds in the affirmative.

Gwendy pulls in a deep breath, lets it out. Sheila takes a bite of her donut and stares intently at the radio monitor, the expression on her face unchanged.

"How in the world are you so calm?" Gwendy asks, breaking the silence. "I'm dying over here."

Sheila gives her a dry look, smudges of white powder stuck in the corners of her mouth. "Twenty-five years on the job, honey. Seen and heard it all by now. You wouldn't believe the things I've seen!" She takes another bite of donut and continues with her mouth full. "I'll tell you this, though . . . if you don't stop chewing on those nails of yours, you're gonna have to walk across the street to the drugstore in about five minutes and buy yourself some Band-Aids."

Gwendy lowers her pinky finger from her mouth and crosses her arms like a sullen teenager.

"Sheila, come back," the radio squawks.

She wipes powdery fingers on her blouse and keys the mic. "Right here, Sheriff."

There's a crackle of static, and then: *"I've got a message for our visitor."*

"Roger that. She's sitting right next to me gnawing on her fingers."

"Tell her . . . we got our man."

70

"TURN IT UP, GWEN," her father says, sitting down on the arm of his recliner. He's staring at the television screen with rapt fascination.

"I'll be making a few brief comments," Sheriff Ridgewick says into the tangle of microphones set up outside the station-house, "and then I'll hand it over to State Police Detective Frank Thome to answer any questions."

He flips open a notepad and starts reading. "Earlier today, the Castle County Sheriff's Department and the Maine State Police executed a search warrant on a resi-dence located at 113 Ford Road in northern Castle Rock. A number of personal items belonging to Rhonda Tomlinson were discovered under a loose floorboard in one of the bed-rooms. After interviewing multiple residents of the home, a suspect, Lucas Browne, age twenty, was placed into custody. After receiving permission from the owner of the residence, Charles Browne, age fifty-nine, to search a family-owned cabin located near Dark Score Lake, officers discovered fourteen-year-old Deborah Parker shackled and unconscious inside the cabin's dirt cellar. She has been reunited with her family and is currently receiving medical treatment at a local hospital."

The sheriff looks up from his notepad, the dark circles under his eyes telling the rest of the story. "After an extensive search of the property surrounding the cabin, officers were able to locate the remains of Rhonda Tomlinson and Carla Hoffman buried a short distance away. Both families have been notified and the victims' remains will be transported to the Castle County Morgue in due course pending further investigation. Lucas Browne has been charged in the abductions and murders of Miss Tomlinson and Miss Hoffman and the abduction and torture of Miss Parker. Additional charges are pending. Lucas Browne remains in custody at this time at the Castle County Sheriff's Department. Detective Thome will now take your questions."

Sheriff Ridgewick steps away from the makeshift podium and stares down at the ground.

"Well." Mr. Peterson sighs. "Far from a happy ending, but it's the best we could've hoped for I suppose."

"Those poor families," Mrs. Peterson says, making the sign of the cross. "I can't even imagine what they're going through."

Gwendy doesn't say anything. The last eighteen hours have been a whirlwind—and her brain and body are still struggling to recover.

Earlier in the afternoon, the sheriff confided in her with great detail the horrors they'd discovered inside the Brownes' house and cabin: a pair of Ziploc sandwich baggies found under a second loose floorboard in Lucas's bedroom, the first containing assorted jewelry belonging to Lord-knows-how-many-women, and the second baggie containing fifty-seven teeth of various shapes and sizes. In the cellar of the cabin, they found a macabre toolkit consisting of a selection of bloodstained pliers, an electric drill, and several power saws. Gwendy wondered how long it would take for the press to get hold of this information.

"Good for Norris Ridgewick," Mr. Peterson says, still

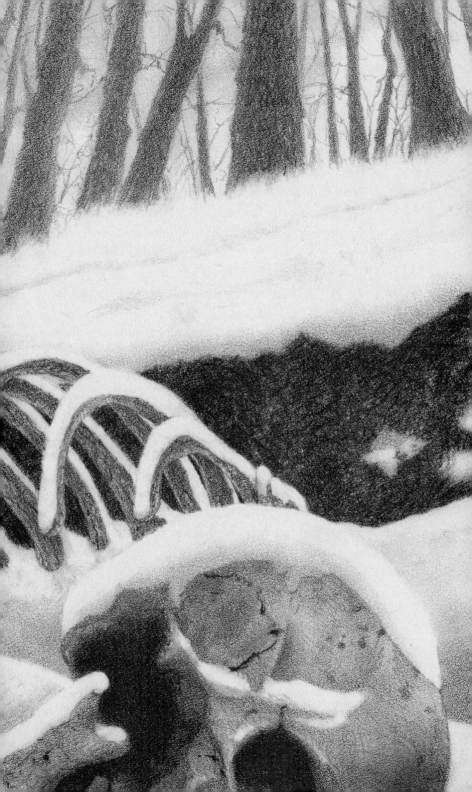

staring at the television. "About time the people in this town gave him his due."

Gwendy's cellphone rings. "I better take this." She gets up from the sofa and walks into the kitchen. "Hello?"

"Got a minute?"

"Were your ears burning, Sheriff?"

"Every day for the last two weeks," he says, wearily.

"We just watched a replay of your press conference. You did well."

"Thanks." He pauses. "I still feel strange not mentioning your part in the investigation. Feels wrong to get all the credit."

"I figure a lot of that credit is overdue around here."

"I wouldn't say that."

"I would."

"I do have one question for you."

Here it comes. "What's that?" she asks.

"I know the whole dental school thing tipped it off for you. And the cowboy boots. But how did you *really* know?"

Gwendy doesn't answer right away. When she does, her words are carefully chosen and as honest as she can make them. "It was just a strong . . . feeling. He gave off this seriously creepy vibe, a kind of *hunger*, you could feel it wafting off him."

"So you're saying it was . . . gut instinct?"

She can picture him rolling his eyes. "Something like that."

"Well, whatever it was, I'm grateful. You saved that girl's life."

"*We* did, Norris."

"Are you home right now? I want to drop off the report I just finished writing. Make sure we're on the same page."

"I'm at my parents' house, but I could swing by the station after dinner."

"That'll be too late. You mind if I bring it by there?"

"That's fine. I'll be here." And she thinks, *If he tries to shake my hand, I'll just tell him I'm coming down with a bug, better not to touch me. Just like I told my parents earlier this afternoon.*

"Great, give me fifteen minutes."

But it only takes ten.

Gwendy is leaning across the dining room table, looking for a corner piece of the latest jigsaw puzzle—the nighttime skyline of New York City—when the doorbell rings.

"That's Norris," she says, getting up from the table.

"Make sure you invite him in," Mrs. Peterson says.

Gwendy walks into the foyer. "You must have been speeding—" she says, swinging open the door. The words die in her throat. "Ryan?"

Her husband is standing on the porch, a bouquet of flowers in one hand, his camera bag in the other. His face is clean-shaven and tanned, and his eyes are twinkling with nervous anticipation. He looks like a little boy bouncing on his heels and grinning.

"I know how you like surprises," he says.

Gwendy squeals with excitement and throws herself into his arms. He drops the camera bag and picks her up with his free hand, spinning her around. Her lips find his, and as he twirls her around and around on the porch of the house she grew up in, she thinks: *There's nothing bad in this man, only* home.

71

FOR THE FIRST TIME in her life, Gwendy wants to tell someone about the button box.

She glances over at Ryan in the driver's seat. She hates keeping such a big secret from him—*any* secret, for that matter—but she worries that it could be dangerous for her husband to know about the box. She also doesn't like the idea of him not having a choice in the matter. If she decides to tell him, he's stuck with the knowledge—and the responsibility—whether he wants it or not. How is that any better than what Richard Farris has done to her? Twice now!

"Penny for your thoughts," he says, checking his rear-view mirror and signaling to change lanes. "You're awfully quiet. Worried about the emergency session?"

She nods her head. "Yes." And it's the truth.

"You'll do great, honey."

"I honestly don't even know what I'm supposed to do, what my role in all this will be."

"You'll listen and learn, and then you'll step up and lead. It's what you always do."

She sighs and stares out the window. Frozen ponds and farm buildings, snow-swirled into gray ghosts, blur past in the distant fields. "Hopefully we can talk some sense into the man. But I'm not holding my breath."

"If I know you, you won't rest until you do."

The call came in the night before. On the other end of the

line was the Speaker of the House himself, Dennis Hastert. His message was brief and to the point: both the House and Senate would reconvene on Monday, January 3 at 9:00 AM, five days ahead of schedule. Gwendy thanked him for the call and hung up and then told Ryan. They'd only left her parents' house a couple of hours earlier, and he hadn't even had time to unpack his bags yet.

She was afraid to leave the button box inside the safe at the condo—what if Ryan decided to go home without her at some point and he opened it?—and Castle Rock Savings and Loan was closed because it was Sunday, so she had no choice but to take the box along with her.

As soon as that problem was solved, another complication rose in its place: because of the short notice, she was unable to arrange for a private plane out of Castle County Airport and was forced to fly out of a larger commuter airpark just south of Portland. But the extra drive and the inevitable questions from Ryan ("Since when do we fly private?") were worth the hassle if only to avoid the X-ray machines at the airport.

"How about I drop you out front with the luggage?" Ryan asks, steering the car off the exit ramp and onto the access road for Portland South Airpark. "I'll go park in the garage and meet you inside."

"Sounds good. We should have plenty of time."

Ryan pulls up to the section of curb marked UNLOADING ZONE in front of the main building—unlike the Castle County Airport, this place actually has more than one, not to mention multiple runways and a three-story parking garage—and unloads the luggage from the trunk, including Gwendy's carry-on containing the button box. He leaves Gwendy standing at the curb and drives across the street to the garage.

She looks around and sees two large families waiting in

line with their suitcases at Baggage Check (in this case, a makeshift fiberglass booth with a pair of oversized grocery carts parked beside it). Several young children are doing their best to squirm out of their parents' grip, and one little girl, her face beet-red and stained with tears, appears on the verge of a major tantrum. A lone, harried-looking airport employee is ticketing the mountain of expensive luggage with the efficiency and speed of a sloth. If he has any help on this second day of January, it's currently nowhere in sight.

Gwendy sighs, feeling sorry for the guy, and sits down on a nearby bench. She arranges the three large suitcases in front of her on the sidewalk and places her carry-on next to her, resting an arm atop it for safekeeping.

"Excuse me, madam, is anyone sitting here?"

"Not at all," she says, looking up. "Feel free to—"

Richard Farris is standing in front of her, looking almost like a mirror image of the man she'd first met twenty-five years earlier on a bench in Castle View Park. His face hasn't aged a day, and he's wearing dark jeans with a button-down dress shirt (light gray this time instead of white), a dark jacket as if from a suit, and of course that small neat black hat of his is perched atop his head.

"How . . . where did you come from?" she says in a low, awed voice.

He sits down at the other end of the bench, smiling warmly. The carry-on suitcase rests between them.

Gwendy thinks about pinching herself on the arm to make sure she's not dreaming, but she's suddenly afraid to move. "Was that you at the mall with my mom? Did you . . . why did you leave the box with me again?" She's speaking fast now, weeks of frustration and anxiety surging into her voice. "I thought you said—"

Farris holds up a hand, silencing her. "I understand you have questions, but my time here is limited, so let us palaver for a spell before we're interrupted." He scoots a little closer to the center of the bench. "Regarding the return of our old friend, the button box . . . let's just say I found myself in a bit of a jam and needed to tuck it away somewhere safe for a short time." He looks at her with discernible affection in his light blue eyes. "You, Gwendy Peterson, were the safest place I could think of."

"I guess I'll take that as a compliment."

"As it was intended, dear girl. I told you long ago, your proprietorship of the button box was exceptional the first time I left it in your possession. And I have full trust it was once again."

"I wouldn't be so sure," she says. "I was a mess the whole time. I didn't know what to do. Push the button, not push the button." She lets out a long breath. "In the end, I did the best I could."

"And that's all one can ask for in any such endeavor. Knowing you as I do, I believe you did quite well this time around, too." He rests his hand on the carry-on suitcase, drumming his long, slender fingers along the zipper. "Ignoring the temptation of the buttons is a difficult chore during the best of times. Not many are able to resist. But, as you well know by now, when left alone, the box can be a strong force for good."

"But I didn't leave it alone," she says with a whine in her voice she remembers well from adolescence. "Not completely. I pulled the lever . . . a lot."

Farris nods his head ever so slightly.

"Will my mother be okay? The chocolates cured her, didn't they?" And then almost as an afterthought: "I had to try."

201

"Hospitals have been known to make mistakes, particularly when it comes to those pesky blood tests. Samples get contaminated; glass tubes get mislabeled. Happens all the time. I trust you left her with a sufficient supply?"

"I did," she says, sounding like a guilty teenager.

A minivan pulls to the curb in front of them. The side door slides open and a woman and young girl climb out carrying suitcases. They both say cheerful goodbyes to the driver, the door slides shut, and the van drives away. The woman and girl walk to the back of the line at Baggage Check and never once glance in their direction on the bench.

"What happened with Lucas Browne and my friend's husband . . . the awful things I saw in my head . . . the box did that, right? Was it because of the chocolates? Will it happen again?"

"That's not up to me. When it comes to the button box, some things—*many* things—remain beyond my reach."

She gapes at him. "But if you don't know the answers, then who does?"

Farris doesn't respond, just studies her through squinting eyes that appear almost gray now. The hat lays a thin line of shadow over his brow. Finally, he says: "I do, however, have one resolution for you that I believe you've been anxious about for quite some time now."

"What?" Gwendy asks, and the whiny tone is back. The idea that Richard Farris is not, in fact, the omnipotent force behind the button box's power, but rather some kind of glorified *courier*, not only pisses Gwendy off but also terrifies her.

He leans closer, and for one tense moment, Gwendy fears he's going to reach out and take her hand. "Your life is indeed your own. The stories you've chosen to tell, the people you've chosen to fight for, the lives you've touched . . ." He waves his hand through the air in front of his face. "All your own doing. Not the button box's. You have *always* been special, Gwendy Peterson, from the day you were born."

Gwendy forgets to breathe for a moment. She feels an enormous weight crumble from atop her shoulders, from around her heart. "Thank you," she manages, voice trembling.

Farris cocks his head, as if listening to a faraway voice. "Alas, my time is up. Your husband is on his way. Lovely man he is, too—a storyteller in his own right."

"What about the box?" Gwendy blurts.

"Already taken care of."

She looks at him, momentarily confused, and then she picks up her carry-on bag and gives it a shake.

It feels empty. It *is* empty.

"How did you—?"

Farris laughs. "You should know better by now than to ask such silly questions, young lady."

It feels strange to be called "young lady" by a man who appears to be roughly the same age as she. Then again, every minute of this experience feels strange, almost dreamlike.

"I must go," he says, standing, and Gwendy's certain he's going to take out his old-fashioned watch from the pocket inside his coat and check the time—but he doesn't. "Although I slowed his progress quite a bit, your husband's a dedicated man and he'll be here shortly." He looks down at Gwendy with that same glimmer of affection shining in his eyes. "And then the two of you shall check your bags and soar up and away into a long and prosperous and happy life together."

"If we ever make it through that line," Gwendy says jokingly.

"What line?" he asks.

She looks up and points. "That one." But now there's

no one waiting in front of the Baggage Check booth. Not a single person.

"What the . . .?"

When she turns back to the bench, Richard Farris is gone.

She gets to her feet and looks around—but he's nowhere in sight. The sidewalk and road are empty. He just vanished into thin air. But not before leaving a goodbye present for her.

Sitting on top of Gwendy's carry-on bag is a very familiar small white feather.

72

"ALL SET," RYAN SAYS, jogging across the street. They pick up their suitcases and head down the sidewalk toward Baggage Check.

"What took you so long?" Gwendy asks.

"Elevator was out of order. Had to walk down three floors. Then I realized I'd forgotten to lock the damn car, so I had to walk all the way back up again."

Gwendy laughs. "My little worrywart."

"Learned it from you," he says, sticking his tongue out at her.

She puts a hand on his arm, stopping him, suddenly serious. "I was thinking about what you said. In the car."

He gives her a questioning look.

"You were right," she says. "When I get there tomorrow, I'll listen and learn, and then I'll do the work. Whatever it takes. However long it takes."

He leans close to her so their foreheads are touching. "Now that sounds like the Gwendy Peterson I know."

"How may I help you, folks?" the smiling man sitting inside the booth asks.

"We're on Flight 117," Ryan says, checking the paperwork.

"Scheduled to take off at 3:10. We'd like to check three bags please."

The man picks up a clipboard and scribbles something on a sheet of paper. "Can I see your IDs, please?"

Ryan pulls out his wallet and shows the man his driver's license. Gwendy fishes her license out of the side pocket of her purse and slides it across the counter. The man picks it up, double-checks the name, and then hands it back to her. "That'll do it," he says. He walks out from behind the booth and places their bags into one of the oversized carts. Unclipping a walkie-talkie from his belt, he keys the button and says, "Flight 117 baggage pick-up. Come and get 'em, Johnny."

A muffled voice answers, "Copy that, boss, be there in a flash."

Gwendy and Ryan start walking up the sidewalk toward the main building, but Gwendy turns back after a couple of steps and returns to the luggage cart. She throws her empty carry-on bag in with the others. Then she reaches into her coat pocket. "Here you go, sir. Happy New Year." She tosses something to the man inside the booth.

He reaches up and snags it. Staring down at the shiny silver coin lying heads-up in his palm, his face brightens. "Hey, now, thank you very kindly, ma'am."

Gwendy laughs. She turns around and takes Ryan's hand and they walk into the airport together.

ACKNOWLEDGMENTS

BEV VINCENT READ THE earliest version of this short novel and, despite his busy schedule, supplied invaluable feedback in record time. Bev also kept the secret and calmed my nerves on a near daily basis. Billy Chizmar read that same early draft and emailed me from his college dorm room in Maine with some simple advice that made the backstory hum a lot smoother. As usual, Robert Mingee caught my last-minute mistakes and cleaned me up for public viewing. Brian Freeman and the good folks at CD did what they always do when I disappear into my writing cave for weeks at a time: they took care of business and let me focus on the words. Ed Schlesinger of Simon & Schuster came on board at the eleventh hour and his insightful notes undoubtedly made *Gwendy's Magic Feather* a better book.

I'm indebted to all of these fine people for their wisdom and encouragement. Just remember, I'm old and stubborn, so any mistakes you stumble upon are mine and mine alone.

I also want to thank artists extraordinaire Ben Baldwin and Keith Minnion for returning for another round and giving such beautiful life to Gwendy's story. I put Gail Cross of Desert Isle Design through the ringer on this project and, as usual, she came through with flying colors.

Much appreciation to my agent Kristin Nelson for all her hard work on this book and for always asking "What's next?"

Finally, I'm immensely grateful to my friend, Steve King, not only for his generous and thorough edit of *Gwendy's Magic Feather*, but also for trusting me to return to Castle Rock and Gwendy Peterson's life.

RICHARD CHIZMAR

ABOUT THE AUTHOR

RICHARD CHIZMAR IS THE co-author (with Stephen King) of the *New York Times* bestselling novella, *Gwendy's Button Box*. Recent books include *The Long Way Home*, his fourth short story collection, and *Widow's Point*, a chilling tale about a haunted lighthouse written with his son, Billy Chizmar, which was recently made into a feature film. His short fiction has appeared in dozens of publications, including *Ellery Queen's Mystery Magazine* and *The Year's 25 Finest Crime and Mystery Stories*. He has won two World Fantasy awards, four International Horror Guild awards, and the HWA's Board of Trustee's award.

Chizmar's work has been translated into more than fifteen languages throughout the world, and he has appeared at numerous conferences as a writing instructor, guest speaker, panelist, and guest of honor.

Follow him on Twitter @RichardChizmar or visit his website at: Richardchizmar.com

ABOUT THE ARTIST

KEITH MINNION SOLD HIS first short story to *Asimov's SF Adventure Magazine* in 1979. He has sold over two dozen stories, two novelettes, an art book of his best published illustrations, two story collections, and one novel since. Keith was a book designer and illustrator from the early 1990s to the 2010s, and also did extensive graphic design work for the Department of Defense. He is a former schoolteacher, DOD project manager, and officer in the U.S. Navy. He currently lives in the Shenandoah Valley of Virginia, pursuing oil and watercolor painting, and sometimes even fiction writing.